ALABASTER
VASES

PRAISE FOR *ALABASTER VASES*

This skillfully crafted suspense story of a police chief tracking a serial killer will have you on the edge of your seat. Readers will root for Josie as she struggles to do the right thing, not only in her relationships, but as she searches for answers about God. Catherine Finger has created a feisty heroine in Chief Josie Oliver as well as a cast of fascinating supporting characters. Looking forward to Catherine's next book in the series.

—**Patricia Bradley,** award-winning author of *Shadows of the Past*

Move over Kinsey Malone, Josie is in the house! This police chief is not only a local leader, but respected throughout her community of coworkers, friends, and good neighbors. She manages to overcome personal challenges while still putting the bad guy behind bars and reconciling her relationship with the "magnificent being." Cliffhanger ending makes you want more!

—**Elizabeth Martin Stearns,** Waukegan Public Library

As a pastor I rarely see characters in books or on screen who wrestle with God in a way that feels like what I see every day. *Alabaster Vases* is the rare exception, a world where spirituality is real but not easy, where the tragedies and triumphs of life work together to form a cohesive whole. I recommend it to anyone who has wrestled with God ... and loves a good mystery!

—**Gary Ricci**, pastor of New Hope Christian Community in Round Lake Heights, IL

The Glock-toting, heel-wearing, justice-driven heroine in *Alabaster Vases* had me from the start. Unrelenting action and witty dialogue kept me loving this ride-along, until the very last page. I strongly recommend this book.

—**Joseph Sugarman**, chairman of BluBlocker
Sunglass Corporation

CATHERINE FINGER

ALABASTER VASES

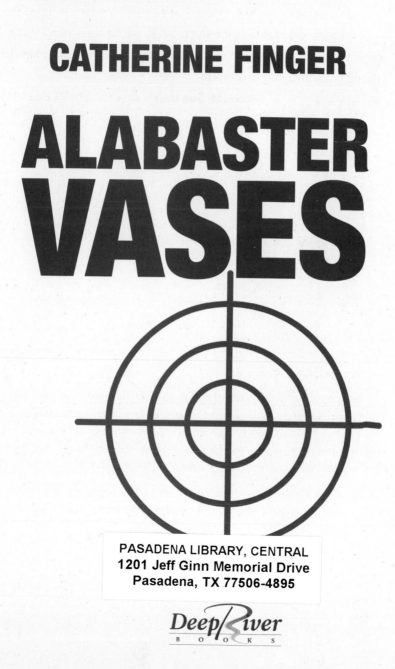

Deep River
B O O K S

Alabaster Vases
© 2014 by Catherine Finger

Published by Deep River Books
Sisters, Oregon
www.deepriverbooks.com

This book is a work of fiction. Names, characters, and events are products of the author's imagination or are used fictitiously. Any resemblance to actual persons, living or dead, is coincidental.

ISBN—13: 9781940269429
ISBN—10: 1940269423

Library of Congress: 2014954326
Printed in the USA

Cover design by Robin Black, Inspirio Design

"We are not antique collectors;
we are not vase admirers;
we are those who desire to smell
only the fragrance of the ointment.
Without the breaking of the outward,
the inward will not come forth."
—**WATCHMAN NEE**

DEDICATION

To the One Most High—*my* Magnificent Being.

CHAPTER 1

Traffic was smooth sailing on I-94 northbound, freeing my thoughts to wander through the murky caverns of my husband's mind. His hands gripped the wheel like a corpsman gripping a jump seat handle a second before the free fall begins. We surged ahead over snowy Wisconsin roads, his large hands quivering.

"Del, please slow down. It's snowing pretty hard out there."

My breath quickened involuntarily. I hated that I reacted like this every time I risked voicing my needs. My stomach clenched and my temples tightened.

He rolled his eyes and shook his head. "Oh, so now you're telling me how to drive too? I don't *think* so."

He never looked at me, and his hands didn't move as he punched the accelerator, rocketing the car to well over eighty on the slippery highway. I prayed to some mythical god that we'd make it intact to the exit up ahead, clenching my teeth and sinking into silent compliance once again. We'd just made it to the turnoff when my cell phone buzzed. I closed my eyes. The misery between us pressed in on me.

"Oliver." I fidgeted with the seat warmer as I answered, my voice flat.

"Josie?"

"Yeah. Hey, Nick." The sound of his voice lifted my spirits, transporting me back to the day we met. I'd been assigned to be Field Commander when we were rangy beat cops together in Chicago. We were young, foolish, and thought we knew it all. Other than me staying close to home and him going on to take one undercover assignment after another until he morphed into a Fed, not much had changed. I smiled looking back, but in the next moment I stiffened as my body slammed into the door panel. Del was taking this corner dangerously fast. I shut my eyes again and concentrated on Nick as the car jetted forward. "What's up?"

"We got another vic. And they're getting closer to home. This is *not* cool." His silky voice hardened as he spoke.

"What do you mean? I thought you said the last murder happened in Spokane. That's not exactly next door. Was this one as bad?"

"Worse. And I'm talking about the next tragedy, not the last one. This one happened last night, early this morning technically, in Mad Town. Popped up on VICAP right away. You on the road right now?"

"Uh-huh."

"You with the man?"

"Does it matter?"

"It matters to me, Josie. *You* matter to me. He's not driving, is he?"

"Yup."

"He knows you're talking to me." It wasn't really a question, but I answered it anyway.

"Yup."

Nick, at it again. My marriage should be off-limits. I loved the man beside me—wounds and all. Even if no one else did. Even if doing so made me almost as sick as he was. *Am I sick enough to stay? God, I hope not.* "Give me some info. How did the killer get from Spokane to Wisconsin?"

"Who knows? We haven't exactly cracked his travel schedule, but everything else is right in line. He grabbed a woman— a church mentor. She'd been working with a six-year-old girl for the past year. Successful woman. High-profile attorney. Not an enemy in the world. Everything to live for. And everything about the kill says it's our guy."

"Please tell me they found traces of drugs. Any kind of tranq in her system?"

"Not a one. She was most likely awake through the worst of it. He's escalating, getting more twisted. And now he's traveling between each kill. We're on high alert, and we want you in our inner circle. We need your hunting skills. Let me sketch it out for you."

Del glared at me and then looked back at the road, his hands clenched. Anger glimmered in his eyes. Why had I given up that once-in-a-lifetime career offer with the Feds tracking notorious criminals? Now Nick had all the glory—and all I had to show for it was Del. I listened to Nick, pinpricks of light sparking through my mind as he revealed the brutality of another innocent woman's death at the hands of this twisted man.

I waited until he finished with the grim details, and then I exhaled hard and fast. I sucked in fresh air as he described the horror of the woman's last minutes alive. I knew Del could sense my discomfort. Was he going to start hammering me again over why I'd married him and stayed in the bush leagues by marrying a local beat cop instead of marrying Nick all those years ago? I couldn't tell what he was thinking any more. When had I stopped trying?

He smiled darkly and waited until I ended the call to act out. "That your big-shot boyfriend again?" Del's menacing tone sent a cold wave of nausea through me.

"He's not my boyfriend. There's been another murder. It ain't pretty." I closed my eyes, gently shaking my head.

Nick and Del had never been close.

CHAPTER 2

We crested a little hill and hit a patch of ice. I entered two worlds—the fantasyland of wishing I were wrapped in the safety of Nick's arms and the agony of being trapped in my car with an out-of-control husband. Del's jaw went rigid as he battled the wheel. I gripped his thigh, but he shrugged me off and grunted.

I chose him—the man in my car—over the man in my head. Why?

The Toyota slid, and the traction system took over, making its own adjustments, trying to keep the car safely moving forward. All the average driver had to do in theory was reduce speed and allow the automated steering system to take over. Del had never been average. He panicked when the car moved of its own accord and punched the gas instead of the brake. The jerky acceleration and his wrestling match with the steering wheel sent us sliding down a steep incline.

Nick's handsome face appeared in my mind, abruptly pulled down like a shade and then ripped away by a fiery-faced Del, screaming beside me as we slid down the hill. White-hot fear swept through me, melting my lips together, shoving words back down my throat before they reached my tongue. I kept my mouth shut, knowing all he had to do was let up on the gas, ease up on the steering wheel, and let the computers adjust the skid.

Instead, he kept accelerating and forcing the wheel in the opposite direction. I thought of my friends, my job, my horse.

"Del, ease up. Take your hand off the wheel for just a second. Relax." I spoke to him in quiet tones, trying to soothe him out of his black mood as he spun the wheel back and forth. We continued to slide down the icy embankment.

"Shut up, Jo! We're locked in a skid! I'm not your pretty boy FBI agent. I know how to drive! There's nothing else I can do!"

His tone of voice sent me plunging deep within myself. Part of me wanted to take control and fix it, but another part of me wanted to walk away. There was a little girl in me wanting to be held, to be cared for, and she just sat there as if in a trance. I knew, we both knew, there was plenty he could do, but instead of acting, I leaned into the little-girl me and hoped he'd calm down. I gave it all over to him and to any god who'd listen.

I tried to pray, but my words seemed selfish and hollow. I wasn't really sure I wanted to be saved to go through this again. So I sat there, holding onto the passenger door armrest with my right hand, bracing the other on the dash, shaking. I did *not* want to die like this. I took a deep breath from a place of strength and peace and steeled myself for what might come next.

I let out a sigh of relief when we finally reached the bottom of the hill with a jolt—sideways, but intact. We ended up on a farm road beside a large field, heading into a little stand of ancient pine and oak trees. I looked over at Del. First, a stony, impassive look came over him, followed quick as lightning by a hideous mask of anger. I was in deep, deep trouble.

He punched the accelerator again, letting up on the wheel long enough for the thing to self-correct, until we were parallel to the road, moving along the dirt path, hitting pothole after pothole.

He sped up. We might've been okay if he would have just kept driving straight. An old farmhouse rose above a ridge a few miles beyond the end of the path.

A glimpse of Nick, smiling, flashed through my mind. Then the sweet smell of Samantha's hair as she rested next to me during a longer-than-usual Sunday sermon. A heavy regret rushed in on the wake of the memory. Why hadn't I pushed past Del's resistance and adopted the foster girl anyway? I wanted a child of my own. A child of my heart.

Del accelerated even more, pushing the Toyota to over seventy miles per hour on the rocky, frozen dirt. He snarled at me and turned the wheel sharply to the right, heading the nose of the car toward a thick patch of mature trees on my side of the road. This couldn't be happening. He wouldn't. He couldn't, could he?

He steered the car straight toward the trees, zeroing in on a large, sturdy trunk, standing maybe thirty feet high, thicker than a tractor tire. I tried my best to relax into it, bracing for impact as best I could. The violent jolt of the fender hitting the massive trunk barely slowed us down as the car slammed into the tree, tearing into my passenger door. Airbags deployed and metal folded like foil, but the Toyota's steel frame protected me like a mama bird folded around her brood. I was shaken, but not too badly harmed.

"My nose! I think it's broken!"

Del's shrill screams stunned me. His side of the car hadn't been touched, though his airbag had deployed. He was shaking theatrically, near tears. He got out of the vehicle, limping. He never once looked back at me, never once tried to help me get out of the wreckage, never once asked if I was okay.

The car door on my side was shredded. The handle wouldn't budge either way. I threw my shoulder into the door and instantly felt a shard cutting into my shoulder. Disoriented, I kept trying to open the door. Blood seeped through the outer layers of my clothing and dripped onto the car seat. Fine, white powder from the airbags settled, revealing blood on the dashboard in front of me.

I unclasped my seat belt, pushed myself back from the wrecked dash, and freed my legs from under the console. Del barked orders into his cell phone as I hoisted myself over the console toward the open driver's door. Once he ended the call, our eyes locked, and for a split second he gave a triumphant smile.

I had to get out of my marriage—the sooner the better—if I wanted to get out alive.

CHAPTER 3

I grabbed the wheel for leverage, and the car lurched to the right, throwing me back down onto Del's heated seat. I sat back, panting. Thin streams of blood dropped onto the warm leather from my jacket sleeve. Pain knifed through me with each heartbeat. Fuzzy stars ebbed and flowed in front of my eyes. I pressed my right hand into the crimsoned leather seat and grabbed the steering wheel with my left hand to steady myself. The ballasting powder from the depleted airbags smoldered against the palm of my hand.

My stomach lurched at the acrid stench dominating the car's interior. I blinked my eyes several times to stop the dash from moving toward me and receding back like a molten sea at low tide. The radio crackled on, comforting me with the low-slung voice of some female crooner.

Strength sputtered through me. I turned off the radio, and then I opened the console and jammed my hand inside, searching for my cell phone. My fingers bumped into a checkbook, a brush, and a pack of gum before grasping the plastic cover. I pulled the phone out and slid it into my coat pocket. I took in another deep breath, closed my eyes, and edged myself to the door with glacial slowness over the warm seat to the door. My left foot hit the ground, and I turned my hips to wrench my right leg out of the car. I pushed myself up. Vertigo rocked me from side-to-side as

I staggered onto the dirt road. Del's face was bathed in blue light when the first squad car responded to the accident.

I tapped the first picture in my faves list with shaking hands and waited for Nick to respond. Del's anger steamed from both eyes. Icy wind battered my matted hair. We locked eyes, and a rogue tear trickled down my face. I stabbed at it with my bloody, right hand. Nick answered, and I turned away from my husband.

"Another Josie call. Miss me?"

Relief flooded through me. Tension eased out of the muscles at the base of my neck. I closed my eyes and breathed lightly into the phone.

"Josie? Whatever it is—I got you."

"Come. Nick, I need you to come get me. Now."

"You still in Wisconsin?"

"Yeah. At the end of the road with Del. He just ran the Toyota into a tree. On my side of the car. By accident . . . maybe . . . maybe not. Just come. Please."

"Cops there?"

"Yeah."

"Don't worry. I'll find you. Then I'll find Del."

<hr />

Nick waited for me at the emergency room registration desk, his jaw tight. "So it's true?"

I nodded.

"Cops say you didn't file a report. Didn't give a statement." A fierce tone bubbled out of him.

I lowered my eyes, shame flaming through every square inch of what was left of me. I stared at the floor.

"And you let them put you in an ambulance with him?"

I shrugged. Welcoming waves of my new, best friend—Vicodin—lapped up my anxiety nicely. Things struck me as almost funny. The neat stitches sewn into my shoulder reminded me of a nice butter braid. That made me hungry. But I smiled and suffered in silence.

"Let's get out of here so you can rest, and we'll talk about this later." Nick's voice felt like warm apple cider.

I started jonesing for a pumpkin sugar donut and decided against mentioning it. Instead, I leaned into him, managing to stay awake as we stumbled together through the parking lot. He opened the door and gently lifted me into his car. His earthy scent wafted above me as he leaned over to buckle me in. I inhaled his welcome scent and smiled before drifting off to sleep. *Safe.*

 **CHAPTER 4**

The killer, wiry and strong, appeared and disappeared like lights flickering in a storm. He started out as a harmless presence in my dream. Sometimes a solid form, sometimes a whisper of a man—always floating above and circling what looked like playgrounds.

He circled far away from the women and children chattering happily below him. But then his circling would grow urgent, morphing into a tangible cloud of malevolence. His mouth spewed filth as he descended, distorting his features. He pulled himself closer to the unsuspecting children and women with each spiral. Close enough to touch them.

Heart pounding, I tried to warn them, but I couldn't speak. I couldn't move.

When I finally managed to croak out a semblance of a warning, the little girls turned with one face, and I wore my throat raw with a silent scream. *I knew her.* All the women turned to look at me, their eyes chilling me to the bone. They were all a different version of me. The killer still circled, coming nearer and nearer, evil coating and coursing out of him like boiling mercury. Mercifully, I woke up. Alive and alone.

Disturbing images hung like wisps of spider silk in my mind. I sat up slowly, willing myself to remember, to make sense of the frightening, now receding, scenes. I shook my head to clear it—a bad move. The pounding in my temples rivaled the pain that wracked my body, especially on my right side. An encounter with a Mac truck would've been welcome right about now. Anything to kill the pain.

It took me a good five minutes to remember I wasn't in my bed. The mule deer rack hanging on the wall in front of me wouldn't have been my first choice of wall art. Even in my painkiller-induced fog, I comprehended I was still in Wisconsin. Alone. More or less. Nick's leather jacket hung on the door of the adjoining room. The door was slightly ajar, and an Italian aria floated into my room from his. Mystery solved.

Del had rented another room last night after the "accident." So had Nick—right next to mine. Equal parts relief and regret accompanied this memory. I swung my legs over the edge of the rickety, resort bed, wishing for the thousandth time that I had a normal marriage. Or at least a safe one. I knew I was better off without Del, especially this morning.

Gruesome bits and pieces of my nightmare bubbled up as I thought about Nick and his immediate response last night. Memories of the Toyota sliding down the hill and slamming into the tree tangled up in my mind. Accident? Intentional? I just didn't know. Details swam in a school of conjecture when I tried to dissect the traumatic event, transforming the images into an inky pool. No. I couldn't go down that path. Not with a killer to catch. I pushed the repugnant thoughts aside to focus on the Little Sister Serial Killer.

What motivated him? We needed to find the key to his choice of victims in order to stop him. Nick's report jarred me, and I still couldn't make sense of it. His description of the crime-scene photos merged with snippets from last night, oppressing my spirit with a weight that would've taken Atlas down.

Something about what Nick had said about this latest murder niggled at me. A connection about to be made hovered out of reach, teasing my subconscious. Something about why the governor wanted me involved in this case. Why me? A small-town police chief.

I'd let it settle in and bubble up when the time was right. Long ago, I had learned that much about my inner workings. There'd been many times over the course of my life when I felt and saw things in my mind's eye before they actually occurred.

Endless nights of poring over reports, witness statements, crime-scene photos, and psych evals had strained me to the point of breaking two years ago while slogging through mounds of data during a spree of gruesome murders. Another one of Nick's "consult jobs." I'd given up the Feds forever ago, but that didn't stop them from asking for my help occasionally. Every now and then I'd get an offer I couldn't refuse. My world tilted more off kilter with each savaged child. I sat beside each and every grieving parent, soaking up clues, tones, and possibilities. Desperately racing an unknown killer, I had nearly joined my colleagues in defeat.

Until my dreams wove into my daytime musings. Jarring bits and pieces from my dreams pressed against me until a pattern emerged among the pictures in my head. Some old-world wisdom buried deep inside led me to the pattern that unlocked the rituals the killer had been playing out over and over with his victims. It led us to his door . . . before a sixth child was taken.

I'd come to trust this inner wisdom, even if I couldn't explain it. All I had to do was go about my business, relax into the rhythm of a new day, and the wisdom would find me. The idea of a relaxing rhythm led my thoughts straight back to Nick.

I'd reached out to him last night, and he was there. He had my back. I fixated on his handsome, square face above a steaming mug of his perfectly brewed French roast coffee. The old familiar longing tried to settle in. I had to knock it off before I started seeing apparitions of the guy wearing my apron and bringing me breakfast in bed. And maybe bringing me my Glock, fully loaded. The man knew his way around firearms.

A shower might help. I wanted hot water washing over me for a good, long time before facing what lay ahead. I grabbed my iPhone and decided to listen to my voice mail before hitting the shower. Speak of the handsome devil.

Nick had already left three messages, telling me in the last one that he was coming next door to pick me up, citing the name and address of our destination for the day. I recognized it immediately. I called him back, and he told me Governor Burke wanted to see us as soon as possible. Since I had no car except Del's, Nick said he'd drive.

I knew he wasn't buying my bravado, but I couldn't worry about that now. I was too busy worrying about what I might have said or done to him while under the influence of some pretty hefty painkillers. Vague images of him bending over me with warm, loving eyes plagued me. Had I kissed him? Lord, I hoped not. Did it count if I couldn't remember it? The only thing I really knew for sure was that at some deep level, I sort of hoped I had kissed him. Sort of. Mostly not.

My cheeks warmed and I bent my head, not liking what I was thinking and feeling. *I am not going there. I'm a married woman. For now.* That much I knew for sure.

What I didn't know was how Nick had been selected for this assignment. The FBI only called Nick in when they were up against a multi-state monster that only the best could catch. I prayed there was some logical explanation, instead of some outrageously skilled killer, that had drawn Nick to this case. His top-flight law enforcement experience maybe. How he'd landed in Washington as some sort of secret agent after Special Forces had their way with him was still a mystery he kept from me. That was how Nick rolled. All I knew was, now he was FBI.

Given that I knew very little about his career trajectory, him being assigned to meet with Governor Burke, *et al,* this morning seemed like one more "tell" to me, but who knew? I had my own connection to the capital, but it wasn't that big a secret.

The killer's dirty work in Wisconsin had both sides of the aisle in the state's capital in an uproar. Governor Burke himself wanted to meet with the core team, and by executive order, that now included me. Nick wanted to give me a pass when he saw my condition last night, but I wouldn't hear of it.

No doubt knowing I'd been summoned to the governor's office with Nick had fueled Del's early morning absence. Which beat last night's ugly scene at the hospital when Nick had showed up in the emergency room. Del's angry bellow had been the only warning before he rushed Nick, completely forgetting his supposed injuries. Orderlies had jumped in and grabbed Del's arms while Nick stood by my side, steely eyes burning into my husband with disdain. When the orderlies muscled Del out of the room, Nick just shook his head and made a tsking sound with his tongue.

I'd been glad to be on the road to la-la-land on high quality, hospital-strength painkillers. Last night it seemed to do my marriage a world of good. Might've just been me though, come to think of it. I tried to shrug with my one good shoulder, dismissing the conflicting thoughts about my two main men as I made my way to the bathroom. It wasn't my best move of the morning.

I'd forgotten about my punctured shoulder, but I remembered it as soon as I shed the T-shirt I'd worn to bed and shuffled over the thick, shag carpet. The throbbing nerve signals in my shoulder muscles felt like hot pokers, and I gasped as I undressed. Not caring that water and bandages don't mix, I was desperate to wash my hair and get presentable before meeting with the brass later that morning.

And I was surprised to realize I cared what Nick thought of my appearance. I managed to wash my hair and protect the bandages. Somewhat. It took a lot more hopping than I'd have liked, but it was definitely worth the effort.

Once I finished my morning routine, I searched for Del, hoping to confront him before I spent the day hunting killers and holding politicians' hands with Nick. I found my husband in the resort's main restaurant, eating breakfast and holding court with a small horde of locals. As I limped into the room, he was giving fantastic, faux details of the accident, making him out to be the hero in some wild, fabricated, man-against-nature adventure.

So this was how it was going to be. Again.

Disgusted, I chose to ignore the whole lot and sat down by myself at the other end of the counter. They knew who I was. They took Del's lead and ignored me. Another set of silent witnesses to my not-so-secret misery. Until Nick walked into the diner, singing in Italian and smiling with his perfect, white teeth.

Nick Vitallero was as gorgeous this morning at thirty-six as he had been at twenty-six. No, scratch that. He was actually *better* looking. A touch of gray at the temples set off his jet-black hair. A perfectly formed, square jaw framed his museum-quality,

Italian features. And I couldn't help but notice he was as danger-ously fit as ever.

Oh, boy. I'm gonna need another Vicodin. STAT.

I ordered eggs and toast and pushed Del and his new buddies out of my mind as Nick slid onto the stool next to me. He winked at the waitress. She smiled at him expectantly.

"What'll it be, Hon?"

"I'll have what she's having with a side of you for supper. Say, about nine o'clock tonight?"

She rolled her eyes, snapped her order book shut, and moved off, still smiling.

"Gotta hand it to you, Nick. You still got it."

"Yes, I do, Jo. I've got everything but you. Which was painfully obvious last night. You didn't have to alert every local yocal within a hundred miles. You called me. That was enough. I would've been happy to take care of you. And Del."

"I couldn't not call it in. You know that. I forgot what it was like in a hick town. I should've thought about the fact that some-thing like this would be the biggest event this side of the state fair for those guys. Why do you think I blew this pop stand the min-ute I got out of high school?" The levity I forced into my voice wasn't working. Nick's face was an angry wall.

"And you bring the keystone cops to the scene from four counties and don't tell any of them about that scumbag of a hus-band of yours?"

"Sarcasm is beneath you, Nick." I reached over and patted his hand.

He nodded thoughtfully. "Maybe so. But anger isn't. You grew up with half of those guys. As many times as you and your friends outran cops during your own crazy years, and you couldn't pull one of them aside and tell them the truth? I guess I should be glad that I'm not the only one you won't let behind those thick walls of yours." He turned his hand over and wrapped his fingers around mine.

"I'm doing the best I can, Nick. And no—I wasn't about to come clean to my old pals. Stealing for-sale signs and getting hauled in to the station together thirty years ago doesn't exactly make them my soul mates. There's no way I'd ever broadcast my wreck of a marriage to those dudes. Heck, three of them went from being tossed into the back of the squad to driving it within months of me taking the oath." I chuckled at the memory.

"It certainly didn't hurt that your sheriff responded to Del's call. The minute he showed up, Del went gentle as a kitten. Made me want to punch him in the face." Nick's casual tone clued me in. He always grew unnaturally quiet when he was jealous.

"You know Quinn and I go way back." I gently tugged my hand out from under his. "Can't say I didn't love the way he bee-lined over to me, completely ignoring Del. I know that was practically worth the price of admission for *you*," I teased.

"No, it wasn't. But standing next to him as he greased the skids by calling the hospital after the medics had done their best to patch you up and drug you down certainly was. He's too good a cop to buy your 'accident' explanation, but even in your weakened state, you charmed him into skimping the report. You were like two little kids laughing about old times in the back of that ambulance, lights on and sirens off. It was ridiculous." He snorted in laughter, and I knew I'd won him back.

"I plead temporary insanity. I was in a very happy place on those painkillers. I found my Sheriff Quinn to be both amusing and a perfect gentleman." I stabbed at my sausage and looked up at him.

"Someone had to chaperone you two. I had to defend your honor. Keep it from turning into a redneck reunion." He laughed again and shook his head.

"Laugh if you must, but it did get us to the hospital in record time."

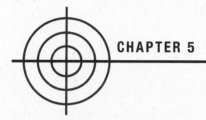

CHAPTER 5

I'd barely made it back to my room to grab my belongings before Nick's distinctive knock sounded at my door. I stood on the other side, trembling. As much as I thrilled at the thought of pulling in the traces with him and going after a killer together, I dreaded being alone in his car all day. I'd resorted to painkillers as an excuse for my sketchy behavior earlier this morning, but I'm not sure Nick even heard me. He'd been intent on wolfing down eggs and giving Del the stink eye.

Being alone with him again without all the distractions unnerved me. His laser mind would cut through my denial of Del's motivation in the accident. Even as we hunted a killer, I knew he'd chase down the truth about my crumbling marriage. Was that really what I wanted? To share with Nick the latest chapter of my gruesome, love story gone wrong?

I was sick of bearing secret agonies. Sick of living in isolation with nothing but the weight of my shame to rely on. Sick of slogging through the dregs of my unhappiness on my way out the door every morning, tiptoeing home every evening and praying I'd make it through another day. Mostly though, I was sick to death of what was true about me and my abusive husband, and I was ready to find a new life. But I wasn't sure Nick could guide me to the truth I sought. I stood there, unable to open the door.

I peeked through the door's peephole to the outside deck.

"Hey, beautiful! Do I have to invite myself in?"

Opening the door, I stood aside to usher him in. He pulled me into his arms as soon as he crossed the threshold, mindful of my bandages. I leaned into him. He tightened his grip around my waist and back, pulling me closer. The feel of him, the smell of him, the solid truth of him comforted me. Regret weaved in and out of my mind for a moment. I was a painfully married woman. He was my best friend. And long ago, he'd once been far more. But I couldn't think about that now. I pushed gently away from his embrace, reaching for some balance between us.

"Thank God you found me last night." I sighed.

"I've never lost track of you, beautiful, and I never will. Don't you know that yet? After all these years? Honey, you're always in my scope."

"Nick." His name poured off my lips like a smile. The warmth and safety of his arms set fire to a potent mixture of raw emotions. My heart went into overdrive, and my windpipe constricted. Every cell in my body thrummed with a distant sense of pleasure. So refreshing after my failure of a marriage. I wanted to be loved . . . not abused.

I dropped my eyes to the porch decking outside my motel door as a wave of guilt washed over me. Should I even try to conjure up the courage to talk about what was happening in my shipwreck of a marriage, or was that way out of bounds? As much as I respected Nick's opinion, mostly I just wanted an escape.

Nick's appearance on the doorstep of this raunchy, rundown, little motel in the middle of Wisconsin Dells could be a sign. Was someone above looking out for me? I caught myself hoping my life could be bigger than this lousy moment in time, bigger than another wounded night by my abusive husband's side. I wondered if I could possibly have a guardian angel and if I even believed in them.

One thing was for sure though—if I had a guardian angel, he was Italian, and his name was Nick.

CHAPTER 6

Olive skin wrapped the muscle of Nick's right arm like water over solid rock in a Colorado river as he navigated the curved road one-handed. Judging by the slow upturn of his perfectly sculpted lips, he must've felt me watching him. I tried to pull my eyes away and content myself with staring out the window, but there was nothing to see but black-and-gray blobs speeding by as we glided down I-94 South toward the capital.

He cracked a crooked smile, pulling me back into the moment. "You shoulda married *me*, Josie. You could watch me all day long." He sounded serious.

My smirk and an eye roll were all I had to offer. We'd been down that road—half joking and half serious—many times before. We'd come closest to the altar years ago when we made it through our first, few, nerve-racking years as inner-city beat cops. He was my whole world once. Until he walked out on me with no explanation, leaving me keening for him like a she-wolf night after night for longer than I wanted to admit.

Then Del waltzed into my life. Del with his Midwestern roots, non-stop charm, and souped-up, black Mercedes. I didn't need to invite the fantasy in this morning. I needed more than the fantasy. I needed Nick next to me in the line of fire. So I managed to remain all-business, giving myself extra credit for keeping my feelings for him on a low simmer.

"Yeah, yeah, shut up and drive."

"That's what I love about you. No guesswork."

"Nope."

"Every man's dream."

"Yup. Well, turns out not *every* man's dream."

"So, are you ready to talk about it?"

"Guess not." I really thought I was, but once we were alone and driving along a quiet highway, I wasn't so sure. I couldn't give voice to this. I couldn't speak the words that needed to be said. Instead, I kept staring at his wrist bone as he drove. Smooth.

Nick moved his hand toward me slowly and rested it on my shoulder. "Josie, there isn't anything you could tell me I haven't already guessed." He widened his fingers and massaged my neck.

Warmth from his hand poured over me, crashing up through my gut where it was met with a roiling sea. Heat rolled up my throat to my face. Twinkling pinpricks appeared before my eyes, and my chest slammed into my lungs, leaving me gasping and confused. I sat in silence, willing my body to come back to me. The car had stopped moving. Nick had pulled into a rest area, and I hadn't even noticed.

He unbuckled his seatbelt and turned to face me. "Josie, what happened between you and Del? What's really going on?" His voice was low and steady.

A tear rolled down my cheek, and I turned to look out the window. I put my hand over his, kept my eyes focused on a fence post and began to speak.

"Shortly after we were married, a couple of months maybe, we were driving on this very highway, fighting. The funny thing is, I don't even remember what it was about. We weren't even really fighting about anything, but we were fighting. And he was driving way too fast, like he does. And all of a sudden, going way over the speed limit, he pulls the car into one of those wayside stops. Without warning.

"I've got cast-iron nerves, but I can still taste the bitter fear that came over me that day. He slammed on the brakes and sent the car skidding to a stop. He was shouting. I don't even remember what he was saying, but he was shouting."

I paused, watching two small girls walking a dog through the dirt toward the designated pet area. They didn't seem old enough to read. How old did you have to be to read these days anyway? Nick kept his hand steady on my shoulder. His rhythmic breathing calmed me. The strongest urge to turn around and lean into his arms overtook me. My heartbeat raced, and I kept my eyes trained on the fence post, taking deep breaths and counting backward.

"And when the car was finally still, the next thing I knew, he was grabbing me by the shoulders, hard, shaking me, yelling at me, saying crazy things. I was so shocked, I didn't even respond. I think that made him madder. He shrank away from me, but he kept yelling. And then he pulled his heavy set of keys out of the ignition and threw them. Right at my head. They hit the edge of the passenger window hard enough to crack it. And that's what stopped him.

"He got out of the car, still yelling, wanting me to drive for some reason. I reached over and closed his door, and then I locked him out. I didn't even think about it, I just locked all the doors."

I drew in a deep breath and held it as long as I could. My face was hot enough to fry an egg off of, and the pulsing of my heartbeat in my temples was an out-of-control bass drum set.

"He got so mad that he started kicking the doors in. Put a dent in the passenger door of his brand-new Mercedes coupe. Something snapped inside of me, and I did something really wrong that day, Nick. Something I've been ashamed of ever since."

I finally turned glistening eyes to face him.

He cupped my face in his hand, and I read the heartbreak in his eyes. "What did you do, Josie?"

I locked my eyes on his, feeling the unleashed shame leak away. "I let him back in."

Twenty minutes later, we were back on the road, bottles of water in hand and the talk of all talks momentarily behind us. I loved that I'd finally broken the dam, but that was all I could handle for today. Probably for tomorrow too. I decided to steer us back to something I could talk about and breathe at the same time—the murders.

"So, why me?"

"What do you mean?"

"Why include me in this investigation? I mean, I appreciate the professional courtesy, but why are you bending the ear of a small-town police chief to help you solve a murder one state over? What's up with that?"

"You've got a good nose for this kind of stuff. You're one of the few people I know with the both the guts *and* the brains to track a killer like this, and to help me find the connections between the kills. We've been talking about it since the murders started, and your gut hasn't failed me so far. You were the first one to wonder out loud if these cases were connected. You were the one to notice the little girl factor. And since the FBI's second-best solve rate is off on another case, I'm sticking with you. Despite the fact that for a brilliant woman, you sure can be slow on the uptake sometimes."

"That's a lot of maybe there, pal. Could be we've seen one too many bad movies. Could be we're making up connections where there aren't any." I wasn't about to ask him to cut me any slack or remind him I wasn't exactly a hundred percent today.

"I don't think so. This case, the Mad Town Massacre, as the press is already calling it, is singing. Loud and clear. It's the same guy. And there's plenty about it that you're not going to like, my friend."

"Such as . . ."

"You're catching the killer's geography, right?"

"Huh? Geography?" His deep sigh seemed legit, and a wiser woman would've stopped there and thought it through. I barreled on. "What do you mean by 'geography'?"

"Last murder. Spokane, right?"

"Sure, not too far from where my sis lives. I haven't forgotten. So?"

His uncharacteristic eye roll seemed like a clue, but I didn't know about what. I might've picked up on it had I not been suffering from last night's trauma. "So . . . Madison, new crime scene, same perp?"

"Yeah, I know. We're headed there now. So?" I shifted uncomfortably in my bucket seat.

"Didn't you go to school in Madison for a day or two? And you've just admitted your small-town ties to the gov." He gestured to me with his right hand, completing his sentence in true Italian fashion.

"See, now that's exactly what I'm talking about. Don't you think that's a bit of a stretch? My nearly one whole year at UW Madison and a family member in Spokane does not a crime nexus make. And I've gone to high school or college with lots of people. That means nothing. You need to admit it. You missed me and drew me into this to get the opportunity to sharpen your skills. Just like the good ole days." I leaned over and playfully punched his shoulder.

He snorted and smiled, ignoring my comment as he soldiered on. "So, is it safe to assume you have neither a plan nor any ideas to offer up along with our condolences when we meet with the grieving governor in a little less than an hour?"

"Condolences? As in on behalf of the agency? What condolences?"

Nick's energy shifted at my question. He stared straight ahead for a good two or three miles, and when he finally spoke, he kept his words measured and slow.

"There are a few anomalies in this case I thought you might have already discovered."

"Yeah? Go on."

"This one hits pretty close to home." He sighed and eased up on the gas.

"As in Madison? Because I went to high school with Governor Burke? That kind of close to home? Is that what this is about? Me being an old high school classmate of Mark's? Really?"

"No. There's more to it." He was quiet. Too quiet. He pulled over onto the side of the highway, put the car in park, and turned to face me.

My throat dried up like a summer canyon. My shoulders sagged, and my head started to ache. "I don't understand. What are you trying to say?"

"The last victim. It was Mark's wife, Josie. Mindy Burke is dead."

CHAPTER 7

The low rise of the marble stairs curved around an alabaster statue on the third floor, and I stood on the first step looking up at it in wonder. The last time I'd passed through this antechamber, I wasn't interested in the priceless works of art. Nick had saved a congressman in a mysterious but heroic way in a distant land that he preferred not to talk about. I had served as Nick's date as he stood before the then governor to receive accolades and honors. I remembered the fish and the dessert being in equal parts amazing at the banquet that followed the decoration ceremony.

The vision of a wonderful dinner party sure beat focusing my whirling thoughts on the disaster I'd been drawn into. My eyelids felt like anvils, and my legs refused to match Nick's long stride. The painkillers I'd popped earlier slowed my thoughts, allowing me to savor the anger and fuel my commitment to bringing the killer down.

"I hate to interrupt whatever party's going on in your head, beautiful, but we need to nail down who's playing which role in about thirty seconds." Nick had stopped on the second landing, waiting for me in my sluggish state to catch up.

I started at the sound of his voice. He noticed.

"Looks like someone's a little on the edgy side. This isn't exactly your first rodeo. Why are you so jumpy?" The puzzled look on Nick's face was a rarity.

I smiled, finally joining him on the landing. "Well, it *is* my first federal case, and if you must know, I guess I'm a little nervous."

"It's an investigation like any other. You're great at this. Don't overthink it. Now, are you going first, or am I?" He put his hand on the small of my back and ushered me toward the final flight of stairs.

"Given the way you sped around looking for a parking space, I'd say you should leave the elected officials to me." I stepped ahead of him onto the first marble slab.

"What's *that* supposed to mean?" He passed me effortlessly, sluicing long legs over the stone risers, two at a time, and then paused for effect.

"Nick, we're in the state capital. They're gonna be sticklers on laws and stuff. Particularly on breaking them. Like pulling into your not-quite-legal parking spot today."

"I prefer to think of it as reasonably legal. Besides, I'm FBI. Perks of the job." He reached the top of the stairs and then turned and reached an arm out to me.

The governor's chambers were located on the second floor of the capitol. The hard marble surfaces of the building felt alive with energy as Nick and I strode down the hallway. The door to the governor's office was slightly ajar, and sounds of someone sharing emotional requests drifted through the open doorway. We exchanged glances without breaking stride and slid inside. Plush carpet muted our footsteps, relaxing me enough to look around as I reached the door to the inner office and pulled it open. We stood in the doorway while Nick rapped a few times on the heavy, wooden doorjamb.

Governor Mark Burke stooped over his desk, palms planted on the glossy surface, pouring over an open file while murmuring questions to two uniformed men. He looked up at the sound of the knock and glanced at Nick before locking eyes with me. I wasn't prepared for the zap of pain I felt when our eyes met. I held his gaze and nodded subtly. Even in the midst of his private horror, he winked at me. Force of habit.

We'd been lab partners our sophomore year at Baraboo Senior High School. Didn't seem possible. Just like it hadn't seemed possible that the "high-powered attorney" Nick had briefly described could have been his wife Mindy—my old high school nemesis. I grew light-headed as the realization sunk in. For one long moment I remembered dissecting frogs in biology class during our sophomore year. My best friend Georgi and I tossed a coin to see who would make the first incision. Mark made his frog stand up and recite the Gettysburg address to impress Mindy when the teacher wasn't looking.

The four of us had been inseparable for all four years. After high school, Georgi married Cliff, Mark tied the knot with Mindy, and we all fell out of touch. And after today, I'd still have Georgi and Cliff, and Mark would have non-stop sorrow. Nothing about life was fair.

I knew I was about to learn something beyond horrible the minute I saw Mark's expression. He poured over gruesome, crime-scene photos of his wife's murder. The state police hadn't had the sense to deny him his wish to see them. I swooped in, closed the files, and pushed them gently toward Nick, all the while keeping my eyes locked on the governor.

My friend didn't say a word as I moved to his side of the desk and hugged him with my good arm. His grief engulfed me, and I sagged as I whispered in his ear. "We'll get this monster, Mark. I promise."

He hugged me harder in response, nodding. We sat down and spoke in hushed tones. Nick took another leather chair in front of the governor's desk.

"You can say as much or as little as you'd like, Mark. We can get the story from the state team if you've had enough for today." My voice wavered, my eyes moist.

Nick pulled out a notebook and pen. "Anyway you want it. If you're more comfortable with just Jo, that's okay too. We're here for you, Governor."

"I hope so. Besides, Jo is the only one I can stand to talk to right now. So no, I'm good. I have to share this with you, and I want you to know how much it means to me to have you both personally involved. I need to know I have the best men and women working to catch this monster, and I know I can trust you."

He was a shadow of the man I'd supported during the last election. Grief had taken up residence in him, offering a preview of the havoc it would wreak upon his body, mind, and soul in the coming weeks and months. I willed myself to relax and absorb every detail he was rational enough to share. I slowed my breathing, quieted my internal dialogue, and took out my notebook, sinking into the heavily padded, leather seat. I nodded for him to begin.

"Mindy volunteered everywhere. You know that, Jo. Everyone knows that. She's been involved in the Big Sisters organization since before we were married."

Famous for her passion and poise, Mindy Burke was one of the most powerful fundraisers in the country. She was the Big Sisters' poster child. Had been their poster child . . . and that had made her a target for a psychopath. I pulled my thoughts together, trying my best to focus as he continued.

"Every Saturday morning, she'd bring the girls from Big Sisters with her to volunteer at the Farmers' Market on the square. All last summer, they worked with Festers Flower Farms—you know how she loves her flowers. So when she decided to volunteer with the girls for the Holiday Fair on the square again this year, I didn't think a thing of it. It was the glads that did it."

"The glads?" Nick asked.

"Gladiolas. She had been working with Drew, her Little Sister, selling gladiolas all summer. Drew turned into just as big a flower nut as Mindy. When Festers decided to freeze dry some of their best stock and save the dried bouquets for the Holiday Fair, Mindy and the girl jumped at the chance to turn them into holiday bouquets." His voice trailed off.

I waited for him to continue, moving my eyes past him to the painting of Lake Mendota hanging over the desk behind him. I wished I was kayaking rather than listening to Mark's sad tale.

"The police report said she'd just sold a big bunch of long-stemmed, purple gladiolas to some dark-haired guy with a walker, and she wanted to help him to his car." He drew a sharp breath and stared at his hands for several seconds.

I waited, tears welling up as I pictured the whole horrible scene and the grisly ending.

"They found the walker knocked on its side next to one of the big bunches of gladiolas near the west parking lot of the coliseum. A witness watched her help the guy out of the flower shop, bending over and chatting with him. Gave the police a pretty clear description of the white van she put the glads in. He said he didn't give it a second thought. He saw the whole thing—said it happened so, so . . . *normally.* He never even knew what he was watching. Never thought to call the cops or report it until his wife saw the story on the news last night. Until she turned up . . ."

She'd turned up dead, brutally murdered, skillfully flayed . . . most likely while still alive. I ached for him. He would have seen every photo, read every description, pieced together a second-by-second understanding of the attack that led to his beautiful wife's death. He was in shock.

Mark and Mindy had fallen in love in August, right before beginning their sophomore year, in the last seat of a long, yellow school bus. On the ride home from summer camp. Four giant teenage boys had been firing insults at an effeminate boy seated across from them. He asked them to stop after catching an air-borne lunch bag with his head. Mark flashed between the bench seats and grabbed the hand of the biggest kid as the first punch was thrown, getting cuffed in the head himself. When I turned back to begin the color commentary with Mindy, I saw the soft love shining through her tears. They'd been together ever since. How do you get over that?

I snapped back to the present in time to watch Mark glide smoothly to his feet. Nick and I quickly followed suit. An awkward silence hissed through the room.

"The eyewitness, what happened to him?" Nick was on point. Thankfully.

Mark looked past us, lost in terrible thoughts. He shifted his weight, clasped his arms around himself, and then unclasped them again. "He's in the hospital right now. Within an hour of the story airing on TV, the witness began to receive death threats from all over the state—online and over the phone. And there was more than a little concern that he might harm himself. We don't need any more tragedy to come from this."

We hugged once more before I left the office, Nick in tow.

Our footsteps echoed off the walls, and I shivered at the hollow sounds bouncing around the empty corridors. Snippets of the last moments of Mindy's life soldered themselves to my subconscious, slowing my steps. Nick reached the end of the grand vestibule before me. He turned around to watch me as I treaded heavily toward him, my eyes tearing up. He nodded as I reached him, and we turned to exit the building in unison.

We paused outside and ducked behind a pillar as he pulled out a bag of barbeque corn nuts and offered them to me. I shot my hand out and grasped it, tearing open the bag, and shaking several corn nuts into my palm before handing it back. We descended the steps, passing the bag between us under a canopy of shared silence.

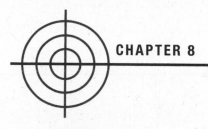

CHAPTER 8

"**H**ow many times has this guy struck, and for how long? And what do you make of the geography? What's driving him? Are there always little girls involved somehow?" I was consumed with a desire to know everything I could about this monster. I'd taken the leap and become convinced of all Nick had theorized. This was a consummate killer, and we needed to stop him before he killed again.

"Here's the thing, we think this guy feels right for a ring of unsolved cases, centering on the islands, but spanning nearly a decade."

"What do you mean, 'the islands'? Which islands?" I turned the bag of corn nuts bottom up, shaking the last few morsels and all the crumbs into my mouth.

"Everybody's dream destination. Hawaii." He kept his hands at ten and two. He could have knocked me over with a feather.

"Hawaii! That's crazy—there's no crime in Hawaii!" I practically screamed the name. It was near the top of my bucket list.

"And there's no shark attacks there either, right?" Nick's half grin was disconcerting. "Nine years ago, a restaurant owner's wife was found dead in the restaurant after hours. She'd been knifed to death. It hadn't been quick, and it hadn't been painless, and there were no signs of drugs at the scene or in her system. That was on Oahu. And she and her husband had just completed the legal adoption of their six-year-old niece, who had been living with them for the past year. The child's natural mother was the suspect from the beginning— messy family case. Three years later, another kill, but this time in Maui."

"Maui?" I was beginning to think there was no safe place on the planet.

Nick filled in as much as he could for me, and even though he held nothing back, the portrait of the killer remained disturbingly elusive. "So, basically, every three years the guy struck again, like clockwork, only on a different island each time. Every murder was unique and had such clear and probable suspects, no one ever made a connection." Nick moved into the Ipass lane and sped under the toll banner.

"So what happened? Did something finally pop on VICAP?" My synapses were firing on all cylinders. I waited for Nick to confirm the inevitable.

"What always happens? He escalated. The ninth year hit, and instead of choosing a victim every three years, he chose four in one year." We blew by the state line as he drove. We'd talked nonstop since leaving Madison, and an hour had already flown by.

"There's not a lot to go on." Frustration edged my voice.

"It's this last victim that has us convinced of the continued connection." Nick shook his head and stretched as he drove.

"What am I missing?" I clasped both hands and stretched them out before me, yawning.

"One murder of a community volunteer with a heart for the nation's youth is sad. Another murder of a community volunteer who loves working with kids in a different state is alarming, but not enough to connect the dots. A third woman in less than four months known for her work with needy girls in *another* state? That got our attention."

"You mean it got the attention of the FBI's Violent Criminal Apprehension Program."

"Like I said."

"So, what's the evidence that's firm enough to put VICAP on high alert?"

"First of all, the age and stage of the victims. Thirties to forties, successful, married, well-known, and much loved in their respective communities. That in and of itself is less common than you'd think. Throw in the fact that each of these women volunteered with young girls in some way or another, as mentors or big sisters, and each of the kids has been six years old, and you've got yourself a pretty solid profile. And the timing fits. Every four months, like clockwork. So far."

"In other words, you've got yourself a serial killer."

"Oh, yeah, and a stone cold one. This ole boy has been at it for a while. He's honed his craft and created a very unique victim profile. With little variation. The only thing we haven't quite figured out is the geography link. Once we do, we'll track him down and cage him."

"Maybe someone who travels for business." I sighed. "Can we stop talking about this for a minute? I'm getting a headache. Pull into the next truck stop so I can get some more barbeque corn nuts, will ya?"

He rolled his eyes and slipped into the right-hand lane, making his way onto the exit ramp. He pulled next to the gas pump and shut off the car.

"All right. But you know the rules. I buy. You fly. And I do mean fly. I want to talk about an exit plan for that violent crime of a marriage you're trapped in, Jo."

His abrupt honesty caught me by surprise. "I can count the times you've called me Jo on one hand. With one finger."

"I know."

I snapped my head around and looked into his deep-brown eyes, unprepared for the compassion skimming the surface as he met my gaze. A tear fell down my cheek, and I glanced away, focusing on opening my door. I looked back at him, offering a small nod, and headed into the convenience store.

Fifteen minutes and a tall cup of really bad coffee later, we were back on I-94, southbound for Haversport. And Nick was back on track. "Your marriage is another murder scene waiting to happen. That's why I can't let this go. It's killing me, watching you let this—let *him*—slowly squeeze the life out of you. This stops now. I mean it."

"I know."

"Which means what exactly?"

I sat in stony silence, wishing he could read my mind. Not wanting to hide it from him, but not wanting to say the words out loud either. Maybe I could wait him out. I'd done it before.

"Not going anywhere, Josie. You gotta talk this time. You know, use your words, as you're so fond of telling Samantha. He wouldn't even let you adopt her. Although why you'd want to subject a child to that sorry excuse for a man is beyond me."

"Look, I don't know what to say without losing the last shred of dignity I have left with you. My marriage is killing me. My husband is killing me. I've got to get out. I know that. There's not a single thing I've done that's made a difference. It only gets worse.

Divorce is the only answer. I know I have to take action, but it's harder than it looks."

This was a lot more than I'd planned on saying, and it made me ravenous. I tore into the bag of corn nuts like my life depended on it. When really, my life depended on getting out of my abusive marriage, and the more I talked about it, the more certain I became. I busied myself with the corn nuts and stared out the window, crunching them in my teeth.

"So what does 'I'm working on it' mean exactly?"

I kept chomping on the corn nuts, shaking my head angrily, as I thought about his question. "I'm working on it, okay? It's complicated."

"Waking up in some fleabag hotel in Wisconsin Dells with a damaged shoulder and a totaled SUV is complicated too. Way more complicated, in fact. You gotta do something. Now."

"You know we just bought that lake-front property. It's the last thing I wanted, and it took every penny of my inheritance, but at least it's keeping him out of my hair. He's spent most of his waking moments over there since the day we closed, and I'm thinking if I can find a way to have him buy me out, maybe I can get a decent settlement and get out fast and cheap."

"Whoa! Are you saying you've already talked to a divorce attorney? I like what I'm hearing."

"No, I . . . I've just been thinking a lot about it. It seems there might be a light at the end of the tunnel."

"You gonna keep the old cabin up north?"

"Oh, my gosh! He hates that cabin. I've actually been thinking about doing exactly that, keeping the cabin and fixing it up. It's got great bones. And it would make a great place for a girl to hide from reality once I get myself in gear and this divorce goes viral."

"Once you get going and leave that pig you married, the press is going to have a field day. One bad cop getting the ax from a police chief? This is going to be the best show in town. I'd book it out of town too, if I were you."

"Yeah, shut up. I don't want to talk about it anymore."

"Okay, your show, your curtain call. But you know I'm here for you."

I nodded.

"I'll shut up and drive now."

"Finally." I grinned at him.

All that talk about the old cabin in the woods had given me a terrific idea. By the time we turned into my driveway, I'd hatched a plan to call my next-door neighbors and initiate a little weekend getaway.

After Nick drove away, I got on the cell, but my fingers trembled as I punched in their number. A cloud of wistfulness and guilt hovered over me. When they didn't answer, I left a message inviting them on an impromptu holiday road trip and then hit END.

CHAPTER 9

The idea of heading up to the old cabin on a lark took off, and my neighbors—Jim and Maggie—had jumped in the car with me. We headed up north the morning after I returned from Madison. Less than three hours later, we arrived in the outskirts of Baraboo, Wisconsin. A short jaunt through town brought us to the old lake road, and in no time we had descended Snake Hill, landing near the edge of a dirt path to the left of the paved road that went around the lake. The dirt path turned into a gravel lane, and *voila*. My home away from home lay dully before us. Jim muscled the lock and sprawled inside. He stepped off the porch and grabbed our bags.

"Are you going to offer this fine man a tip, or am I?" I leaned over to Maggie, pulled a few dollar bills out of my pocket, and winked at her.

She snatched the bills out of my hand. "Oh, Jim, got a little present for you." She rolled her eyes at me and scurried after her husband. "Come on over here you big, handsome man." By her laughter and his guffaws, I surmised she'd stuffed them in his belt.

I grabbed three bags of groceries and headed inside. Twenty minutes later, we had all changed into jeans and sweatshirts and sat eyeing a tray of cheese and crackers. I leaned forward, pushing up my sleeves to fix plates for everyone and pass them around. It wasn't until they were both staring at me that I realized they'd grown silent.

"What? You're not into Cheddar? It's Wisconsin. It's like apple pie up here." I sat back and shoved a wedge in my mouth to demonstrate. They weren't laughing, and they still weren't talking. They were staring at my right arm. I looked down at it and froze.

A faint blue outline of a once large bruise stretched from my right elbow to just before my wrist. Faded yellow colored the inside of the oblong bruise. Color flamed in my cheeks, and I stared at the plank floor.

"The man has got to go." Jim's voice was too low, almost a growl.

"Look . . . I . . ." This was not how I wanted the weekend to start. I couldn't find the right words to convey—what? Anything. There was nothing I could say.

"Jo, we love you. And we will not stand by and watch Del ruin your life. This has to be our weekend. I am declaring this The Weekend. The Weekend that changes everything. Because it has to. You're running out of time. One of these days he could kill you." Maggie got up and came over to sit next to me on the couch. She slid her arm around me, pulled me in to her, and kissed me softly on the cheek. "Jo, I love you. *We* love you. And we're telling you—in love—that it's okay to end this abusive sham of a marriage. We're begging you to end it. You're not safe."

"I know, Maggie, I do. I have to find the courage to take a stand and end this, or fight for it one heckuva lot harder." I picked up a glass of water, lifted by the Packer's logo adorning it.

"Fight harder?!" Jim shouted. "There's no more fighting of any kind, hard or soft. There's only flight. A one way ticket outta there. And it's got your name on it. We'll help you pack. As soon as we get home." He got up and joined us on the couch.

"Great, a Jim-Maggie sandwich." They both leaned in, and we put our arms on each others' shoulders. We sat there for several minutes, basking in the warmth of our friendship. Their support centered my soul and proved to be the perfect start to our time together. Two glorious days later, we headed back home.

I was lucky to have them along. Jim was a wizard with power tools and wood, and Maggie, his wife of nearly fifteen years, had a knack for getting things done. I couldn't believe all that we'd accomplished in almost forty-eight hours. The cabin looked better than it ever had.

On the way home, Jim drove Maggie's Mercedes. He managed to whittle down the three-hour drive from Baraboo to Northern Illinois to slightly more than two. Tired but happy, we decided to invest the extra hour having lunch at the Rocking Horse Lounge, a shoe-box-sized dive with a wood frame and a green roof, sitting just over the Illinois border on the southern-most edge of Wisconsin. During daylight, it looked like a Lincoln log house, except for the big white sign propped up by two large telephone poles. The joint served the best burgers in both states and offered an endless supply of chilled Bud on tap.

Jim loved the place, so Maggie and I bowed to his choice. Which meant nothing but agony for Maggie, my Fortune 500 CEO friend. With her French-manicured nails and sleek, ivory pashmina, she blended in about as well as a kitten at a committee meeting of the Westminster Kennel Club.

I tried to hurry Jim through our burgers and Sharps. "C'mon, buddy, drink up. Maggie's getting restless."

I picked up my burger and looked over at the sole pool table, where a dirty hulk of a guy leaned over the velvety-green slate. Tattoos ringed his left eye. He looked like a biker I had arrested once.

Then the guy had the nerve to wink at me. A small, black snake tattoo undulated on his arm when he crouched down to zero in on the cue ball, all the while staring at me intently.

I removed my badge from my purse and flashed it in Snake Eye's direction so he could get a good glimpse. His expression froze, and then he focused on the cue ball. I snorted and took a big bite out of my burger before turning my attention back to Jim.

His Carhart jacket was still zipped up halfway, probably to keep the cigarette smoke from seeping into the loud, blue, Hawaiian shirt he wore underneath. A movie man by trade, Jim owned an impressive collection of authentic Hawaiian shirts. At an even 6 feet and 180 pounds of lean muscle, he could actually pull it off. The combined impact of his costume choices and special effects could tempt you to underestimate him. And that would be a mistake.

"Aren't you through yet?" Maggie asked him.

"Hey, don't rush me. A man cannot be hurried through the few visceral pleasures of this brief life."

"This is not our final destination, you know. Jo and I want to get home, and we still need to pick up the dogs after we unload tonight, don't forget."

Maggie snapped open a mirror and freshened up her lip color before tossing both the mirror and her lipstick case into her Fendi Sellaria bag and clicking it shut. The sound of her voice charmed him, and he took a last bite of his burger.

"All right, ladies," he said, lifting a French fry, dripping with ketchup. "A toast to the most excellent adventure of the past forty-eight hours at Jo's most excellent cabin in the woods. And to think I spent it with the two most beautiful blondes north of the border."

Maggie and I laughed, fueling Jim. He lifted another French fry.

"And here's to the mysterious, though delicious, decision of Jo's *not* to tell that husband of hers thing one about our little road trip."

"Jim!" Maggie turned to me, looking surprised.

A trickle of laughter snuck out of the side of my mouth. The hint of a smile broke through, and within a few seconds, I was laughing full bore. Jim put his hand in the air, and we bumped fists victoriously, his dark-brown eyes full of mirth. I slapped my hand into his, and when we stood up, he pulled me to him, crushing me into a bear hug.

"First step is the hardest, Jo. The rest will come faster than you think. You can do better. You're gorgeous, you're brilliant, and you're the chief of police. It doesn't get any hotter than that."

He kissed me on the forehead and pulled away. In one swift motion, he smacked a twenty on the table and linked arms with Maggie and me, carting us out the door with him into the chilly evening.

Loose thoughts floated around in my head as we drove through the dark, winding streets on our way home. I wondered how much of their lively banter had been tailor-made for me, my gift from an unseen God wrapping me securely in a blanket of comfort and warmth. I needed warmth and security now more than ever. Deep gratitude flooded my thoughts. Having two such wonderful neighbors was a sweet gift.

We drove into the back entrance of our subdivision, passing the large, Christmas-bedecked homes of friends and neighbors. Maggie manhandled the Mercedes around the curving streets. Jim turned up loud, unfamiliar music as she turned onto our block, and both of our houses came into view.

"Dude!" Jim muttered.

Maggie eased her foot off the gas, dialing down the rest of the evening into slow motion. There was my house, lit up like a Christmas tree. Bright light spilled out into the street, reflecting off the snow back onto the house. Every light was on, walls and floors laid bare, everything so very wrong. Stripped walls showed through undressed windows. Security spotlights focused on empty areas through the windows of my once beautiful home.

Even as my trained eyes drank in every detail, I couldn't immediately comprehend what had happened. The front door stood wide open. Both garage doors were up, and litter blew haphazardly across the yard. My pickup truck was gone. And I heard water running somewhere as Maggie parked the Mercedes in the driveway.

We stepped out of the warm car and stared at the desolate scene. I started toward the house, flanked by Maggie and Jim. Together, we trudged up the front steps of my home like complete strangers. The ornate iron mat was missing from the top of the porch steps. I had nailed it into place with my brand new nail gun two weeks after settling into our new home nine-and-a-half years ago. It must have taken some work to pull it up.

We followed muddy footprints to the front door and paused, glancing at each other nervously. Jim snapped his head to the right and spun around. I followed his lead, wishing I hadn't noticed the wreckage in the yard. More footprints, car tracks, and truck tracks crisscrossed the driveway, spilling onto the lawn. The depth of the tracks and the width of the tires told me a large, heavy vehicle had been parked in the yard at some point over the last two days. Deep ruts branded the snow-covered lawn on the side of the porch. Something large and very heavy had been dragged across my front yard.

The large, front windows offered a detailed view of the chaos. My house lay barren. My holiday decorations had been completely destroyed, festive strands of tiny white lights ripped down, cords dangling. Two small pine trees were missing from the concrete urns by the door. One of the urns was missing too. I could not force myself to move.

Jim swore, and Maggie spoke into my ear, but I couldn't understand a thing they were saying. All my attention focused on the destruction of my home. Maggie steadied herself with a hand against the cedar siding of my empty house, and we stood huddled in the doorway like uninvited guests.

Even the entryway and stairwell walls were bare, and worse, they looked like they'd been punched in spots, drywall pushed in all the way to form dark holes. The stairway walls were covered in what looked like kick marks. I pushed inside to the powder room in the foyer and almost fainted. The warmth of Maggie's presence was welcome at my side.

None of us dared speak now. I numbly walked into my kitchen and had to hold on to the wall to keep from dropping to my knees. This was *not* my kitchen. I felt violated. Muddy tracks marred the once gleaming hardwood floors. Every cupboard had been torn open and ransacked. Some of the cabinet doors had been ripped off the hinges. One of them was completely missing. Another lay broken on the rug by the back porch door. The great room beyond it looked like a war zone—eerily bare, with more holes knocked into each wall. A mad, hungry giant had defiled my home, had roved through ripping everything away from its careful place in my world.

I stood in the remains of my kitchen, dizzy, unable to think. The mottled Corian of my island countertop was covered in smudgy prints. A cream-colored piece of paper rested at the edge of the counter, a page torn from one of my journals. I recognized the writing scrawled across it and felt a surge of anger. Leaning against the counter, I read the note left behind by my husband.

Jo: I filed for divorce on Friday. I have another woman and a very good attorney. Ours is a business arrangement that has come to an end. It's time to divide the assets. You need to get an attorney as I have. Know this, I want the lake-front property and everything I took with me today. And the boat, my share of hard cash, and all the vehicles. If you don't fight me on this, I will leave you alone. If you do fight me, I'll go for everything you have, every penny, both properties, plus your pension, what's left of your inheritance, and your retirement savings. Don't fight me. You can't win.

—Del

Behind me, Jim spoke to the police dispatcher on his cell phone as I reached for my work phone to make the call that would change my life forever.

CHAPTER 10

I punched in the number closest to my heart and squeezed my eyes shut. I didn't breathe until the ringing stopped, and then I sighed in desperation as Nick's voice mail droned on. I opened my eyes and spoke into the phone. "Nick, I need you. *Now.*" And then I hit END.

My second and last call of the evening went straight to my Deputy Chief Lauren Mitchell—Mitch. She was a natural-born leader, and I knew I was going to elevate her to my second-in-command before my first official day on the job. I'm good that way. I can read people. Most people, that is, except for the ones I marry.

Cop to the core, she answered on the first ring despite the fact that it was 2:15 in the morning.

"Chief?" Her groggy voice held promise—a lifesaver tossed straight to me in the midst of the rocky waves of my new reality. I could picture her dark-red hair mussed from sleep. Her husband of three years softly snored in the background. They were just starting out, and everything I saw between them was everything I wanted.

The picture brought me to tears. "Mitch, I have a personal emergency to tend to. Del left me... for good I think." Breathless, every word constricted, I read the note to her, and then I choked out a mini version of the hell I had entered.

"Chief! Do you need me to come over? What can I—"

"Would you please shut up? That's all I've got right now. Look, I gotta go."

"Oh, my gosh! I'm so, so sorry." Her voice was low, and she spoke in measured tones after listening to my ice-cold explanation of events over the phone. "What do you need most from me right now?"

My stomach tightened. I drew a sharp breath and wiggled my mouth to loosen up the muscles of my jaw enough to respond to her. Maggie and Jim stood with their backs to me in front of the fireplace, whispering in low tones as they surveyed the damage in what used to be my great room. I turned away from them.

"I need you to be me. I need you to go into my office in the morning, business as usual. I need you to run the show for me, buy me some time. Just sit in my chair and stay there for the next twenty-four hours, okay?"

"No. Nothing's okay. There is nothing at all okay about any of this. I'm on my way."

"Mitch! Just sit tight for right now. Can you do that for me?"

"I got your back, Chief. Anytime, any place. You just hang in there, and call me when you need me. Anything else?"

"Nope—just thanks, Mitch. Later." I ended the call, my hands still shaking.

Ten minutes later, Nick stood by my side, and we walked through the remains of my home together. I laughed at the sight of the five-hundred-dollar pair of Italian loafers he'd pulled on bare feet under his favorite pair of jeans and white, button-down shirt. His clean silhouette was framed in stark contrast to the chaos all around us as I slogged through every room on my second tour that evening. I stopped short on the upstairs landing and waved

Nick forward. I let him take in the emptied bedroom scenes alone. I didn't need to see those again right then. He swore as he padded softly down the stained, carpeted stairs.

"That pig is going to pay for it this time, Josie." He pulled his iPhone out of his shirt pocket, opened the notebook app, and sat down on the stairs beside me.

"That godforsaken pig cannot get away with this! And who lives in a neighborhood that lets this kind of stuff go on without callin' the cops! Where *is* everyone?"

"Think about it, Nick. It's almost Christmas. We're about the only two families in the subdivision not hiding out on some tropical island. Place is as good as deserted this time of year."

"And, of course, Del would know that. He knew he'd have plenty of time to mess up your house on his way out. You're gonna be so much better off without him. You know that, don't you?"

Tears flowed down my cheeks, and my throat swelled so tight that all I could muster was a hoarse whisper. "I don't know. I just don't know anything anymore." Steel knots roiled in my belly, and I started seeing stars.

"Look, I'm not okay right now. I need some time to pull myself together—to figure all this out. I need you to go home and be your amazing, professional self so I can fall apart. I need some time to see exactly what I'm up against. Might take a little ride out to the lake-front property. We'll see what I need to do next." My voice cracked. I was skating on the bitter edge. Time to go.

"You know I'm here for you, right? But, listen. I have to know you aren't going to be alone. Can I stop by later? Can I send Mitch over? Maybe make this one official?"

"No, honey. That ain't how this is gonna work. I can't deal with that right now. I just need you to step in come daylight. Keep the investigation hot, do your best without me for a few days, and don't call me unless you really need me. You're the only one I want to hear from today, so make sure any case updates go through you. I am *not* in the mood for anything or anyone else today."

"Sure. I'll step away and have your back. But you're not going through this alone. I don't care how tough you are."

"Fair enough. I'll stay with Maggie and Jim, so relax. And I mean it. Other than you and them, I really don't want to see anyone. I sure can't talk about this officially yet. I've got to think things through. That day has come though, trust me. I will make this one official, and we will drag his sorry butt in."

"All right, I'll take off then. And I'll make sure Mitch checks in with you after the 6:00 a.m. roll call." He stepped into my space until only a whisper stood between us. The air came alive with the heat that rolled off of his body onto mine. He lowered his voice to husky. "Josie, I'm here for you. Always have been, always will be."

A crooked grin crept across my face. Who *was* this man? How'd I get so lucky? "Thanks. I'll keep you posted."

He wrapped his arms around me, kissed the top of my head, and held me for several seconds before pulling away. I looked up at him with moist eyes and watched him trail slowly down the stairs. Once he vanished through the broken front door, I used my shirtsleeve to wipe the tears from my face.

I sensed my tears had only just begun.

CHAPTER 11

"Hi, sweetie, ready for some coffee?" Maggie's voice woke me as she breezed into her guest bedroom with two steaming mugs, dressed to the nines for work. It was already 7:00 a.m. Monday morning. Jim would be long gone by now. I hadn't heard a thing since crashing at their place three-and-a-half hours ago.

Monday. Wow. Harsh reality, and I just wasn't ready for it. Maggie pushed the covers aside and sat lightly on the bed. We drank in silence. She took my hand and squeezed.

"Maggie, what happened? He's gone, and he's trying to crush me on the way out. What did I do to deserve this? How could he? How long has he been planning this?" Sobs surged forth, and I was right back on the edge of out of control. "And by the way, this on the heels of the worst case I've ever had the bad sense to get caught up in. I don't know which is worse—my professional life or my personal life. It's one giant nightmare all rolled into one."

"That's it. I'm staying home with you today." Maggie tipped her cup up and drained it.

I sat up to put my mug on the bedside table, strong objections standing at attention on my tongue, but she kept right on talking.

"Resistance is futile. I'm staying with you. I don't want you to be alone right now. We'll face this day together." Her kindness was met by my silence, even though I really, really wanted nothing more than to sit right down and cry for a week. Maybe two. My head hurt so badly, I could barely think.

"Thank you. I don't even know what to do first. But I'm pretty sure I couldn't get to it without you carping at me all day long."

"It's what we do. We *do* for each other. I'm here for you. Now shut up and get some rest."

"Yes, ma'am. But could you at least allow me the courtesy of my one phone call?"

She smiled, triumphant, produced my iPhone out of her suit pocket, and slipped out of the door.

Silence filled the room, and I had the luxury of facing my personal hell undistracted for a few minutes, surrounded at a distance by my loving friends. Half of whom were definitely well armed, locked, and loaded. A glimmer of gratitude pierced the blackness in my mind. I'd been blessed, even lucky, in the midst of this miserable moment.

My relaxed mind poured over my calendar, and I reviewed what I could recall of this week's agenda at the department. There were two personnel issues I knew Mitch could handle easily, along with a scheduled department shoot she could run without me. I had room to breathe, and I decided I was pretty fortunate to be in my fourth year as chief of police in Haversport instead of in my first chaotic year. I'd had the opportunity to put a fine crew in place over the years. Warm pride welled up as I thought about how self-sufficient most of my officers were—well equipped to handle any emergency. More or less.

And Nick was following up a lead on our serial killer this morning. He wanted me to call a divorce lawyer today and let him handle the investigation for now. All in all, not a bad place to be when facing what I was facing. At least my professional world was holding its own while my personal life tanked. Could be worse. There was no big news afoot in our boring little village. No nasty criminals needed to be captured or killed. No ne'er-do-wells on the edge or even seeking refuge at our shiny, new station. No dangerous, deadbeat spouses on the lam—except for mine.

Deep thoughts for my first cup of coffee. I slowly made my way out of bed. Maggie had laid out some jeans for me. She must've gone through my clothes next door. God bless her. Hers would never fit me. She was shapely and petite. My curves were rounder, and all five foot seven of me hung from an athletic frame.

The warmth of the shower spurred me back to life, and I played over the events of last night one more time. My mind wandered down the empty hallways and the broken plaster of my home. The one question I couldn't stop asking myself—*who was she?*—hung just beyond my reach, overshadowed by an equally ominous question. How much worse was this all going to get?

I stepped out of the shower and dried off with a plush, white towel. When I finished, I examined myself in the mirror, wondering which parts of me hadn't pleased my husband and what sort of body had replaced mine. Heaviness crushed me, pushing me off balance, and I sank to the toilet seat, clutching the thick towel around me. I wondered for a split second if I could go on—if I wanted to. I got up and dressed.

I made my way downstairs to the kitchen. Maggie sat in front of the hearth, waiting for me. I sank into an overstuffed chair next to her.

"How did this latest horror start? What *happened*, Jo?"

"There's nothing to tell that you don't already know."

"Did something happen recently that threw him over the edge?"

My heart beat wildly. Red heat rocketed up the small of my back toward my face. My throat tightened, and I tried to keep the venom out of my voice.

"Maggie, I'm telling you, I didn't do a thing. He's the bad guy here. I told you he tried to kill me with his car, and the whole time he had a girlfriend on the side. If he thinks he's gonna take away our dream property, he better have his head examined. I'm taking a road trip out there. Now."

"Do you think that's wise?"

"I'm going. I have to, and I'm going alone."

Frowning, Maggie tried another tack. "Will you at least take Nick with you?"

"I'll think about it. Course, it'd be a lot easier to call him using the latest Bluetooth technology in your Mercedes."

Maggie sighed. "Naturally." She pulled the keys out of her purse and placed them on the dresser on her way to the door.

CHAPTER 12

Driving always calmed me, and driving Maggie's black beauty would get me to the lake and back safe and sound. I'd worry about *sane* later. The Bluetooth chirped. I pressed the little telephone icon on the steering wheel and said hello into thin air.

"Come get me, beautiful." Nick's smooth tones filled the car. "Nick!"

"Just come get me. I've got everything you need, Splenda and all. I'm at the corner of Hainesville and 120. Keeping it hot, just the way you like it."

The smile in his voice thrilled me, and I was grinning like a school girl by the time we finished the call. Looks like I'd have company on the ride into the unknown after all. Three minutes later, I pulled into the Starbucks parking lot. He was waiting for me in his government–issue, nondescript, dark sedan. As soon as he pulled his sleek frame out of the front seat, I could focus on nothing but him. He glided over to my side of the car. I lowered the automatic window and stared up happily at him as he set the coffee down on the pavement by his side.

"Hey, beautiful." He squatted down, leaned into my car window, and gave me a quick kiss on the cheek. Placing his hand on the car door, he offered me the venti life saver with the other.

"Cut the foreplay and get in." I gave him my best cop glare, and he shook his head, laughing. He moved around in front of the car and slid into the passenger seat.

"You know you want me, Josie. Just a matter of time. No worries. I can wait a little longer. Gonna be worth it. Gonna definitely be worth it." He reached for my hair, swirling a lock around those perfectly formed fingers.

"At least someone's in a good mood today."

I kept the faux hardness in my voice, but I knew he felt the glow from within that took me over on some level every time he was near me. Lately, it had felt like a nuclear power plant. My emotions were on overdrive. Energy sparked between us as Nick regaled me with current FBI cases in other places. I found his chatter strangely comforting. Still, as we followed the familiar route west on 120 toward the lake house—my husband's dream house—I fell apart in silence. Nick's hand moved to my shoulder as we drove. I had the presence of mind to switch off the Bluetooth before calling Mitch along the way. I owed it to her to catch her up, and even though I'd filled her in on the basics last night, I poured out the full version of my sad marriage tale to her. I glanced over at Nick, and his face looked grim and angry as he learned even more than I'd told him about Del's abuse.

Mitch's little saltbox of an office must've been shaking from the rafters at the news. She stayed calm, cool, and collected though. And for the hundredth time in the last twenty-four hours, I wondered if everyone but me had seen this coming. No one else seemed all that surprised at my horror show.

"I'm sorry," I said. "This is all so unbelievable, I can't take it all in. I don't know what to say."

"This is a horrible way for your marriage to end. But in a

way, he's done you a favor. There's no decision to agonize over any more. *He* left *you*. It's out of your hands. Wait a minute . . . I hear traffic noise. Are you driving somewhere right now?"

"Take a breath, Mitch. Yes, I'm in a car, but Nick's by my side. I need to check on the lake house."

"Don't do this to yourself. You don't know what he's capable of. Turn back. *Please*."

"I have to do this. I love you. I don't know what else to say. I'll call you. Gotta go." I hit the END button, and Nick came alive.

"What'd she say about us going out there?"

"Very bad idea."

"And you said?"

"We're practically there."

"Great."

I hadn't noticed slowing down during my chat with Mitch, but the speedometer was hovering around fifty now. I slammed my foot on the gas, and the Mercedes accelerated to over seventy. One more light, a left turn, and a country road would bring us face-to-face with the end of my marriage. Numb, I sped through the light and then sat back in the deep, leather seat, preparing myself for what I didn't know.

The house sat back quite a ways from the road—the only thing it had in common with my little cabin in Baraboo. Twin brick towers marked the paved driveway, complete with lanterns and a cacophony of sleeping wildflowers flanking the curved asphalt drive. We pulled in, sailed around the circular drive, and parked in front of the three-car garage. The middle stall was peaked, specially built for boat storage and complete with a porthole-like window in the center of the dormer. I entered the garage door code for the middle door.

Nick touched my arm. "Josie . . ."

I followed his gaze to the snow-covered, gravel path leading to the custom-built boat house, edging the pristine lake below. Parked on the pathway next to the boathouse were two identical U-Haul trucks. Thick layers of frost covered the hoods of both vehicles. A low fog crept up from the ground and slowly washed over me as I gazed at the trucks, confusion mixing with a certainty too raw to soak through.

In unison, we turned back to the garage and noticed it was eerily bare. No boxes, no vehicles. A different sight than the one I remembered on my last visit, not ten days before. Del and I had spent the weekend here. I had painted and wallpapered rooms, delighted to be playing out my ideas on our new home. I had spent a small fortune on custom fabrics, papers, and linens. Doing the work myself was one of my concessions to Del's concerns about spending too much so soon.

Nick took my arm as we walked through the garage together. It was too quiet. I unlocked the door and stepped into the kitchen.

My eyes rested on the custom-built, kitchen table set. Del and I had taken my mother to an Amish colony in Wisconsin this past summer to commission the table and chair set. I'd known the man who built this table since high school. Sitting in the middle of *my* table was a feminine-looking basket that was *not* mine. It was surrounded by gift wrap. Gaily colored ribbons and a card sat on an open Bible next to it—one of my old study Bibles, opened to a passage about forgiveness. The note was to my husband. From another woman.

Every detail of the scene was meticulously frozen and stored in separate compartments in my mind, ready to be taken out and carefully examined in the upcoming days, weeks, and months.

There were two coffee mugs in my sink. One of the cups was stained with bright-red lipstick, hardly smudged, as if the lip impression had been painted on. I picked up the mug and turned it around in my shaking hands to get a good look at the impression on the rim. This revolting evidence jarred me, and the mug fell out of my hand into the sink below, snapping the handle off cleanly.

Deep pain surged through me. My heart seized, my lungs stung, and I sucked in air as white-and-black pinpricks flashed through my mind. I screamed. Then I screamed again, louder. I picked up the stained and broken mug and flung it against the granite floor. The crashing glass as it shattered against the stones suited me. Releasing my anger felt good. I relaxed. Nick put his arms around me, and I stood silently, staring at the broken mug.

We walked down the hall to the unfinished powder room. Someone had moved my hand-painted wooden sign. In its place jeered a plastic-coated, eight-and-a-half-inch by eleven-inch picture of Del looking drunken and seedy, smiling in a way I'd never seen him smile before. Another woman had placed a photo of my husband on my wall in my unfinished powder room. It made me sick to my stomach.

We followed the hallway into the office. Brown-paper grocery bags sat on the desk. A pair of my favorite riding jeans spilled over the top of one of the bags. I stepped forward, touched the fabric, and froze in place. I wanted to see if I could feel *his* presence, or *hers*.

Nick waited for me to lead the way to the master suite. A dresser stood out from the wall opposite the bed. I went through each drawer. The bottom drawer held a woman's clothes, lingerie, candles, and a DVD. A trashy porn. I started swimming in nausea, and I must have doubled over.

Nick came to my side. "Let's go, beautiful. Enough. We've seen way too much already today."

I ignored him and stepped into the walk-in closet. I'd moved some of my clothes in weeks earlier in anticipation of living here full time as soon as our other house had sold. Del had placed my custom blouses in a paper Jewel bag. My evening bags lay haphazardly on the floor. Some other woman's shoes sat next to Del's. Backless, gold, faux-leather with four-inch heels.

I ran to the bathroom and went through every drawer in his vanity, finding condoms on two different shelves. In my own cabinets, I found a fragrance I didn't use. My custom monogrammed hand towels had been yanked off their racks and lay damp and crumpled on the counter. A pair of panty hose were bunched up against the bottom of the cabinet.

I walked out of the bathroom, down the hall, and into the great room. I sank to my knees before the spotless wall of windows. I watched a row of pine trees swaying in the wind. I used to think those pines beckoned me to the lake. Nick joined me without a sound.

I sat there, thinking back to how Del and I had fought for months about buying this oversized, luxury home for just the two of us. Finally, my hefty inheritance from a recently deceased aunt and Del's accusation that I'd never let him have his dream won out. I had reluctantly plunked down every penny I had in an effort to save our marriage by giving Del exactly what he said he needed to be happy.

"Turns out happy doesn't last very long." I realized I'd finished my thought out loud by Nick's solemn look.

I moved my knees under me and grunted to my feet. Now I understood how badly that SOB had manipulated me.

My anger fueled fantasies of catching him in the act with his mystery woman and shooting him in the head. What good would that do me? I'd rather see him brought to justice. If there *was* any justice for what he'd pulled. Probably not. Letting him live and pursuing justice would end up costing me a lot more in the long run than him being good and dead. And his little "friend" too.

The saxophone tones of my work cell yanked me out of my dark reveries.

"Yeah."

"Chief Oliver?"

"Mac?"

"Yeah, it's me. And this isn't a social call. Where are you?"

"Ah, out at the lake house with a buddy, why?"

Silence.

"Is that the best place for you to be right now?"

"Sir?"

"Just . . . look. I need you to drive in. Now. Get out of there. That's not the smartest place in the world for you to be or be seen today."

"Okay, Sheriff. Mind telling me why?"

"I want to make sure we get ahead of the storm before the bottom drops out of this case." Chills crept up the back of my neck, and the pinch of a headache worked its way up to my temples.

"Storm, sir?"

"The storm that Del created. What, you didn't think I'd hear? It's everywhere already. And it's . . . complicated. Come in, and we'll talk."

He hung up, and I stared at the phone as if it were alive. I snuck a look at Nick. He was staring at me, waiting for my direction. The sound of tires on gravel got our attention, and we turned our heads to watch a caterer's van drive past the house, heading down past our house to the water where several other majestic homes lined the lake.

"Let's go. I was hoping to poke around the boathouse, but that's going to wait for another day. I don't want to watch new neighbors happily prepping for a holiday party I haven't been invited to. I've seen enough for one day. Not that I've much of a choice in the matter anyway. That was the sheriff. He wants to get a handle on the PR nightmare my life has become. I'll come back later."

I opened the garage door, and Nick and I descended the four steps single file. He had been a rock, and I appreciated that he hadn't gone ballistic when he saw what Del had done. We pressed on through the expansive garage and reached the Mercedes sitting in front of the garage doors. He held open his hand and I tossed him the keys without question.

"We'll come back later," I said again with a tight smile as he backed the car into a y-turn and nosed the car slowly down the drive.

I turned around in the seat for a few seconds, watching the little shed down the hill recede through the back window. The caterer's van had vanished around the bend. I pulled my eyes away and watched the ground lining the driveway. Bulbs I'd planted in the fall flanked the drive and surrounded both brick pillars. In a few months, they'd be in full beauty. Where would I be by then?

CHAPTER 13

Nick pulled into Starbucks and hurried inside. His way of having me drop him off I guess. He emerged in record time, loaded with two familiar cups of heaven.

"This gonna be enough to tide you over on the way home, beautiful?" He leaned in and handed me the cup.

"You're a life saver, Nick. In every way." I smiled my thanks and he nodded at me, winked, and turned on his heel. I watched him walk away, sipping the nectar of the gods.

By the time I got home, there were three trucks and one sedan parked in my driveway. Maggie descended from my front porch and waved me over. I rolled down the window and looked up at her, confused.

"Maggie?"

She didn't say anything, but the ghost of a smile pulled across her face, and she stepped in front of my house. "You know how I love to decorate. Thought you could use a little help."

My head dropped forward, and my eyes grew wide as I looked from her to my driveway. She waved a hand at me and nodded her head as if to tell me to get out of her car. I stepped out into the cold air.

"When did you have time to do all this, and wait, is that Mitch's car?"

"Could be. I'd go see what the fuss is about if I were you. Now scoot!"

Maggie took the wheel of her Mercedes and headed to her house next door to park. I walked between the two trucks from Saxony's, nodding at the local handyman behind the wheel of the white van. Mitch smiled at me from her village-issue town car and rolled the window down at my approach. She held out a cup of Starbucks and tilted her head at the passenger seat. I laughed as I trotted over and plunked into the warm seat.

We drank in silence for a few moments. I was watching the workers when Maggie walked up to my side of the car. I rolled down the window to talk to her.

Maggie leaned in close as she spoke. "You go ahead and do whatever it is you ladies do in the name of the law. Ms. Mitchell will take you to your meeting with the sheriff. I'll spend the day with these lovely workmen and see what we can do about some home improvements."

"And all that stuff about agreeing with me about not going to work today?"

"Oh, that. Yeah, well, that might've been a bit of a ruse to occupy us long enough for Jim to set this enterprise in motion. I knew you'd want to go and 'man up,' as you say, around your office yet today. Am I right?"

I jumped out of the car, hugged her tightly, and whispered, "Thank you, Maggie."

She hugged me back before turning me toward the car. I raised my hand in thanks as Mitch maneuvered the car around on my ice-covered lawn and made her way to the street.

"What kind of barbarian driving is this?"

"First things first." She raised her coffee cup in a silent salute and drove on.

I nodded. "You know something?"

"Nope. Enlighten me."

"I think I'm gonna survive this mess. I really do."

"That's my girl!" She drove out onto the slick street and stepped on the gas, eliciting warning beeps as the car fishtailed on the ice, and we laughed out loud again.

Mitch reached behind my seat. She pulled out her dress-blues hat and placed it on my head. I was still laughing when I reached out to bump fists with her. I pulled down the visor and played around in the mirror.

"Halfway home, girl. Having a good hair day and a great hat day. Now we'll just have to see about the rest. I gotcha covered." Mitch pointed to the back seat.

I turned around and smiled at one of my dress uniforms still wrapped from the last trip to the dry cleaners. A favorite pair of calfskin designer pumps sat on the seat next to the newly emptied hat bag.

"I owe you one."

"Yup."

Our next stop was Mitch's house. Her husband met us at the door and gave me one of his soul-cleansing hugs. I felt peaceful, hopeful even, in their presence. Mitch opened the powder room door and hung my uniform on the hook. They were quietly talking as I closed the door to change.

I caught my reflection in the vanity, and I was grateful for Mitch's foresight and attention to detail. She'd chosen my favorite, navy-blue wool work skirt. I'd had this uniform carefully tailored until it showcased my five feet seven inches to maximum

advantage. I'd need every little perk I could find to force myself
back into my work routine today.

I was also having a fantastic hair day, courtesy of Maggie's
salon-quality equipment. I'd taken the time to blow out my dark-
blonde hair into the straight and silky look before me. I never
left my bedroom without performing my basic skin-care routine,
donning gold jewelry, and spritzing on a favorite fragrance. I was
pleased to see I still had my morning ritual working for me—
with a little help from my friends today. All in all, not a bad look
despite the tired eyes, tear-stained face, and doomed-to-all-get-
out new life.

I opened the door and stepped into the foyer, ready for anything. Mitch waited with two travel cups of coffee. She handed
me a mug, nodding slightly. I accepted it with a shrug. The aroma
alone was enough to send me into a caffeine high. But that was
the least of my worries. I could cut back on my coffee consump-
tion anytime. Maybe tomorrow.

"Let's roll," she said, as we walked out the door.

The richness of the coffee and the bond between us were all
we needed as we rolled through the streets in our old companionable silence.

We were pulling into her parking spot at the station when
she turned to me. "Chief? You thinking about an attorney yet?"

"Not yet."

"You have to. The sooner the better. You *need* to get a good
lawyer, and you *need* to start making some contacts today. You
want me to get on it for you? Call around, make some inquiries?"

"No. Thanks though. I get it. I know I need to start moving,
and I'll get there soon. I may need you when the time comes. Until
then, let's just walk through that door and get 'er done."

"Roger that, Chief."

Mitch and I walked up the stone steps and stood in front of the back door of the station.

"You sure you're up for this?"

"Yeah, I'm up for it. All I'm gonna do is sneak in, stomp around, and let everyone know I'm alive and well. Perfect timing. Most of 'em should be at lunch by now."

"Good point. So, we doin' this thing?"

"On three," I said, as I adjusted the hat on my head.

We opened the door into a stairwell. Mitch headed downstairs to the shooting range, and I headed up to my office. With any luck, it'd be deserted at noon on a Monday. I pushed the fire door open and stepped into a hallway with black-and-white diamond linoleum. The hall wound past storage lockers, a utility room, and a break room before turning into a smaller, carpeted hallway. Small offices hugged both sides for about twenty feet. A large open area, containing the call center and computer surveillance and conference rooms, stood at the end of the hallway. There were three corridors leading out of the open area, and I took the first right. My receptionist was at her desk in the center of the hallway. Our eyes met as I walked across the soft carpet.

"Afternoon, Chief. Are you here for your meeting?" This was Julie-speak for *"I got your back, Chief."* Her way of telling me she knew everything that had happened in the past twenty-four hours. I dodged her.

"Yeah, hold my calls," I mumbled as I swept past her, shutting the door louder than I'd intended. I wasn't being fair to her, but I couldn't handle our usual banter this afternoon. And I sure didn't have it in me to talk about my ridiculous new lack of a life. Tragedy or comedy? Who knew?

It was all I could do to walk into the building with Mitch like we'd done every day for the past four years, and I was hoping to keep my personal crisis close to the vest. Until I ran into Julie.

She'd been my faithful assistant and number-one fan every minute of every day since I took the position of chief of police. And she was everyone's ideal woman. Youthful radiance and healthy, blonde hair framed cornflower-blue eyes set perfectly into an unforgettably beautiful face. Half the guys in the department were speechless around her. The other half constantly vied for her attention. But Julie was simply Julie—sweet, professional, happily married, and holding us all together day in and day out. She'd no doubt been under Mitch's influence already today. Given my stellar impersonal performance, she'd probably even sent an emergency text message, tattling on me to Mitch.

Whatever. I let my breath out in a long, low stream, bracing myself against the office door for a second. What *was* I doing here today? Oh, yeah, Mac wanted me here. But I needed to be here for me. To have a place to call my own, to keep my world spinning, to get back to my normal life. Guess it wasn't working all that well so far.

Two raps sounded on the door. "Chief? Can I come in?"

"Yes, of course. C'mon in, Julie."

"I just wanted to let you know I'm here for you—if you need anything." She stepped up to my desk as she appraised me. What did she think of my formal attire, fabulous hair, and the deepening bags under my eyes? I should've known she'd be way ahead of me.

"I'm so glad you're here for the holiday party. Commander Mitchell would have done a fine job, but it's you everyone really wants to see. I know you'll be your amazing self, and the families will appreciate your personal attention." And in one smooth motion, Julie pulled me back into my work world. I'd forgotten all about today's party. Thank God for Julie. She had her notebook out and was bound to get me caught up. So I tuned in.

"So far, nothing unusual has come up. I was here for the six o'clock report this morning. York called in sick again. I already asked Hernandez to check it out. Probably not legit, but doubt we'll be able to prove it again." She flipped a page.

"And you didn't miss much last week. Just the usual, not-so-happy holiday domestic calls. Nothing you haven't seen before. All handled by Commander Mitchell. We do still have that three o'clock meeting scheduled to review the personnel investigation results with the mayor. I've already heard from him that he'd be happy to reschedule."

I looked up into Julie's clear-blue eyes, catching the hint of a nod. Her way of telling me the mayor knew about my personal nightmare. And if he knew, everybody knew.

"No, let's keep it. Thanks. And the ceremony's at what, six?"

"Actually, we have it set for four-thirty tomorrow over at the Brown County College conference room."

"What? Why are we at the BCC? I hate that conference room."

"Because it's the middle of winter, and it's the only place that will hold the ceremony unless you want to go back to the courthouse. Do you not remember having this conversation last week?"

"Oh, yeah. It's all coming back to me now. Thanks. Anything else I should know about or remember?" I winked at her and moved around the desk, letting her know we were back to being on the same side again. She was nervous, and I wanted to reach out to her as she'd reached out to me.

She shifted her gaze downward and fidgeted for a moment before she spoke again. "Well, nothing more for today. But you *were* scheduled to be out of town for the next ten days or so, you know." As soon as she said it, I gasped and sat down hard on the edge of my desk. My stomach roiled, and I pictured my living room sofa. My head started pounding. Del and I had planned on spending the holidays at our timeshare in Maui. We were set to leave on Wednesday for two weeks in paradise. Some paradise.

"Yeah, about that."

"I'm just so sorry!" She clasped my hands in both of hers as tears spilled down her cheeks.

"I can't do this right now, Julie. Please . . . leave me alone . . . just for now, okay?"

She nodded her head and stepped out of my office. I sat on the side of my desk for a very long time, watching the shadows grow longer in the afternoon sunlight.

Then I rallied and spent the next few hours reviewing case notes on the Little Sister Serial Killer. Nick was following up on Mindy's murder, and we both feared the killer would strike again. But he wanted me to take some time before leaping back into the case. I tried to release my mind to sift through the notes and make connections, but it wasn't working. And every time I thought about the once-vibrant women dying so horribly, an overwhelming darkness spread through me, rendering me nearly powerless. All I wanted to do was stop. Stop being. Stop doing. Stop existing.

Force feeding myself happier scenes, I wandered into memories of my first ride on my horse Scooter and the exhilaration of winning our first, world-level equestrian event together. But Del had been there, and scenes stretched out and included him against my will. I willed myself to stop thinking about him, making it impossible to think about anything else.

The exhilarating feel of his leather jacket under my eager hands as he tore through mountain passes on his Harley, our bodies shifting and leaning in unison as he navigated switchbacks and narrow roads on our way to the top. The devil-take-all plunge on the way down in the moonlight, my happy screams bursting forth at every surprise in the road on our way toward forever together. The brevity of the mountain top experience we'd shared but could not sustain, no matter how hard I scraped and clung and scaled. A pinnacle reached that could not keep me from the unrelenting plunge down the other side.

Darkness clung to me like mist over a river bed, and my whole body seemed foreign and depleted. I tried to think of happy memories or objects to ward off the pull of this cauldron of emotions, but all I could find was a deepening sense of hopelessness, with a burgeoning side of self-hatred.

Where was this coming from? Maybe I should see a psychiatrist. But who? And how to describe this despondency? I closed my eyes and envisioned a red briefcase with a brass clasp and matching hinges. I visualized picking up the dark thoughts by the scruff of the neck and placed each one in the smooth, leather briefcase. Then I snapped it shut and locked it tight.

I spent most of the rest of the afternoon sighing, staring off into space, and checking my watch. Not the best use of the city's tax dollars, but it was all I had to offer. I had to pull it together for that afternoon's meeting. I dreaded the conversation. One of our finest had been accused of being a little heavy-handed with the jail's "overnight guests," and I was scheduled to share a summary of investigation results as well as my recommendations with the village leadership team.

As much as I wasn't looking forward to the confirmation of inappropriate behavior I was about to deliver about a member of my staff, a feeling of relief washed over me that I finally had to face some bad news that wasn't my own. Beat the stuffing out of the chat I'd have later with the sheriff.

The first meeting went off without a hitch. The most notable aspect of our time together was how difficult it seemed for the three amigos to look me in the eye. From initial review to final deliberations on my dismissal recommendation, we spent less than thirty minutes together. And that included me watching them shift their weight from one leg to the other in long, awkward silences at the beginning and end of our meeting.

If this was how the boys were going to respond to me, I should go through debilitating, personal circumstances more often.

CHAPTER 14

I had just enough time after my meeting with The Village People to call Maggie and catch her up to speed. She kicked it in to high professional gear as soon as she heard the tone of my voice. In a previous life, she'd been a kick-butt personal injury attorney, and she hadn't lost her killer instincts. I listened to her spout off legalese long enough to write down names from her own short list of divorce attorneys. She suggested I call one before the sun set. Today.

Then she dropped a bomb by suggesting I go see a counselor right after I told her about the strange visions and dark feelings I was experiencing. And she had an idea of who she thought I should see. So much for attorney-client privilege. Might as well tell my doctor I ate ice cream for breakfast. Just as I hung up after our conversation, Mitch's customary two quick raps on the door announced her arrival right before she let herself into my office.

"How was your chat with Maggie? She give you anybody good to see?"

"Yeah," I snorted. "Maya."

"Maya?"

"Figures it'll look good for the court case she's sure will come out of this gunfight. Wants me to get right on it—made an appointment for me and everything."

"*You* have an appointment with *Maya*?"

"Yeah."

"You're going to see the she-devil shrink without being ordered to?"

"Yes. No. Well, turns out she'd received a friendly, off-the-record call from the sheriff, strongly suggesting she talk me into it. So much for needing to see Mac today. Took care of that with a quick call too. He wanted to ease me into the idea of seeing someone. A certain someone."

"Was that before or after he called Maggie and told her what to tell you?"

"My point exactly."

"Well, happy holidays."

"Ho, ho, ho."

"When you going?"

"Nine o'clock tomorrow morning. Why not? Might as well get it over with. I can tell by looking at you that this isn't exactly a coffee break. What's up?"

"I've got some good news and some bad news."

"Hit me. Bad news first, please."

"Well, the bad news is, you might want to reconsider the holiday party this afternoon."

"What? Why?"

"It's gonna be a bunch of cops who are on Del's side. He got to them before you did." Her eyes held pain and a hint of embarrassment.

I knew I was missing something, but I couldn't tell what. "Mitch?"

"Del just sent in his RSVP. With a plus one on it. And a smiley face." She spit out all this information, staccato, both eyes riveted to the floor.

"What! Who does that . . .? It's not enough that he's ruining me at every turn. Now he wants to embarrass me in front of the guys? He needs to be taken out!" I tried to conjure up my tough-girl act, but it fell flat and unconvincing, even to me. Especially to me.

The raw pain hung heavy between us, drowning out words and sounds and heartbeats. Every cell of my being felt heavy. "So what's the *good* news?"

"Turns out there isn't any."

"Yeah. I figured. Mitch?"

"Yeah?"

"I can't go tonight," I whispered.

"I know. I'm on it."

"Thanks." I turned to face the library area in the back of my office. Shame burned across my face. I didn't want to look into the face of pity from a colleague—friend or foe.

"Chief?"

"Yeah?"

"You don't deserve this. I can't believe what that rat is doing, and we will *not* let him get away with it. We *will* find a way to see he gets his."

"I know." My voice was in danger of breaking, but I wasn't about to cry in front of her again today. "Thanks. I couldn't get through this without you. It gives me a world of comfort to know you'll be there in my place tonight. Now go and raise some Cain for me, would you please?" My half smile won her over, and she straightened up to go.

Almost as an afterthought, she dropped a bomb of her own.

"Oh, and I've taken the liberty to schedule a little meeting for you before you leave today. With Bruce."

"Bruce? What is it with you guys taking it upon yourselves to set up all these unwanted meetings?"

"Think about it."

"All right, not a bad political call. I get it. Look at me. I'm thrilled. What time?"

"About ten minutes ago. He's sitting outside in the reception area. I haven't mentioned a thing to him, and I don't know whether or not he's heard anything from the rumor mill. All I told him is you have a personal matter you might wish to discuss with him in private. He made himself instantly available."

"He knows."

"Yeah, that's what I figured too. Don't shoot the messenger." Mitch winked at me before turning and letting herself out.

I stepped into the reception area to greet him, and we walked toward my office together.

Bruce Schofield was one of two part-time village attorneys. He'd come up through some unusual ranks. Harvard educated and from a family of tremendous wealth, he'd eschewed it all and gone into the public defender's office for the bulk of his career. We all thought he had political aspirations a mile long, but turns out he just wanted to do his own version of the right thing. We shared a deep and genuine respect for each another.

"Chief Oliver, I'm sorry for your loss. I've only heard a few of the rumors, but I know enough to be extremely sorry. And to let you know if there is any way at all I may be of service or support to you in the upcoming days and weeks, I really want to be."

"Thank you." I turned my head to the side and looked at his reflection in the office windows. He was tall and muscular, neither fat nor slight, and always seemed to be one of those ready-for-action guys. He sure looked military to me, but he'd denied it so often that I kept my thoughts to myself. He was ruggedly handsome and wore well-cut suits. Nothing about him seemed to fit the lowly public servant profile he projected. But then, maybe I puzzled others too.

"Any friendly advice, one village official to another?"

"No advice. Just a little truth. You'll be better off without him in your life. That man wasn't worthy of you. Period. He was an anchor tied to your leg—a fool and an embarrassment to men everywhere, and he didn't deserve you. Everyone is on your side here. Everyone."

"Does it really have to come down to sides? Can't my personal life stay personal? Is there something you're trying to tell me?"

"Your personal life can't stay personal. It's way too late for that."

"What's that supposed to mean?"

"Just that I'm on your side."

"Is there something else you'd like to share with me?"

He looked at me in silence for several seconds and then shook his head. I couldn't read his eyes, but I knew he was hiding something. Something big.

"No. Just that I'm here for you. Anytime. Please remember that."

Something in his voice gave me the chills, and my throat dried up. I stood, offered him my hand, thanked him for coming, and walked him to the door. After his exit, I sat behind my desk in the waning light, wondering what had just happened.

It just kept getting weirder. I stood to put on my coat and shut off the lights on my way out. There was something very unsettling about Bruce's message this afternoon. I wanted to believe him when he said he was on my side. And I *did* believe him . . . until he repeated the same thing. Twice.

CHAPTER 15

Uncertainty hung in the air in Bruce's wake. I didn't feel like staying in the station and risking more face-to-face with anyone today, and I didn't feel like heading to my newly barren tomb of a home. I stood in front of my desk and stared into nothing for way too long before I sat down and flipped open my computer. While waiting for the screen to turn from black to green to action, I fumbled around in my top left drawer and found a half-empty bag of barbeque corn nuts next to a pile of unopened mail. I pulled the mail out and plopped it on the desk.

The first envelope was a perfect square, adorned with the signature calligraphy of one of my dearest friends—Georgi. We'd grown up together. I was by her side the night she fell in love with her husband Cliff over stale beer and bad dancing, and I looked forward to the comfort of their living room. *Soon.* I nudged the bag of corn nuts open, leaving it in the drawer to minimize crumbs, and popped a few into my mouth.

I sat back in my leather swivel chair, enjoying the tangy-sweet flavor as I poked at my iPhone screen until I reached the current files on the Little Sister Serial Killer. Nothing new had come in.

What mysterious force drove this psychopath toward each of his victims? What happened in his early life to drive him to such heinous acts of cruelty? How would his secret past lead us to him in time to stop another murder? I couldn't muster one shred of compassion for this killer. I only wanted to see him captured or killed as soon as possible.

Troubled by the lack of new leads and not wanting to go home yet, I looked at my watch. I had just enough time to stop by and see Samantha during her after-school program, but I'd have to hurry. I raced to the parking lot, pausing only to pull out my phone. Laughing, I punched in the word INCOMING, our secret code, knowing how happy the unexpected visit would make her and hit SEND. I made it there in record time.

Saint Camille Catholic School spanned a city block, though that included the church, playgrounds, parking lots, and a century-old convent. I pulled my squad car to the front of the building, mindful to leave the spot marked FR. HANK vacant. I'd learned the hard way not to mess with him or his parking spot.

The hallways were dimly lit as I walked toward the cafeteria. Student work filled the walls, leaving them awash in the smell of fresh paints mixed with crayons and slow-drying paste. Both wooden doors stood open, letting loose a cacophony of happy sounds to mingle with the art as children's laughter wafted down the halls. I slid through the doors and came to a stop, scanning the room for her. Rectangular tables, seating twelve kids each, had been painstakingly set in place five deep on each side of the room.

Samantha was seated all the way in the back of the room, at the last table, way on the left, as far away from the door as possible. Protecting herself by losing herself in the crowd? Sister Angela was on duty, and she noticed me before Sam did. She was standing next to a statue of Saint Theresa, facing the kids. She wore a full habit, complete with the requisite large, blocky, olivewood rosary.

"Hey, Chief! Great to see you. Are you here to take a snack break with Samantha?" Angela's voice felt like cotton candy, and she flooded the large space with her smile. Sam loved her, and for that reason alone, I'd do just about anything she asked of me.

"I am. I hope I'm not intruding. How much time do we have left? Would you mind if we spent a few minutes together? I probably should have called first. I'm sorry." I was falling all over myself, weak-kneed at the thought of seeing Sam. This version of "Mother May I" usually bought me an extra minute or two.

"As soon as she's done, I'm sure she'd love to show you her art project from this afternoon." Sister Angela beamed.

"I'd love to see it. I enjoyed the lovely pieces you've already posted in the hallway on the way in. Quite a bit of talent resting here before us, I'd say."

"You could certainly say so now, though you might not have said that had you been in the room with us while we made the sausage, so to speak. Elementary art is not for the faint of heart." Her smile never faltered.

I laughed and waved at Samantha when her little head popped up and she noticed me for the first time with a gigantic smile. It took all I had not to run to her and scoop her up, but I wanted her to approach me first. I wanted to let her make all the choices. It was one more step toward helping her heal from all of the other choices that had been torn away from her. I watched impatiently as she packed the trash from her after-school snack onto her tray only to rearrange it, making sure everything was put in the right spot on the right conveyer belt at the tray return—an agonizingly slow routine.

She finished her duties and then walked in measured steps through the cafeteria. For one bright moment, I knew she wanted to run to me, but Sister Angela raised an eyebrow in Sam's direction, and she pulled herself back into a fast walk. She pranced up to me with twinkling eyes. Then she held her right hand out, and I stepped in and took it gently. I waited for Sister Angela's nod before walking her out into the hallway.

Several steps beyond the door, Samantha's little body quivered, and she squealed happily, stepping in front of me to grab my other hand.

"Miss Jo! I love you so much! I'm so glad you came to see me today!"

I knelt down and scooped her up into the gentlest of hugs. "Oh, my darling Sam. I love you too, sweetie. Now tell me about your day at school." I sat back on my heels and smiled as her happy little voice sang out a hundred tiny details of her day. She made me supremely happy, and being with her seemed the most natural, the best, and the most important part of my life.

"I made a cow today in art class. You wanna see her?" Sam's voice was thick with admiration. She loved her cows, and by extension, so did I.

"Of course I do, baby doll. Take me to your moo-dur!" I waited for her laughter to chime in, but she looked at me, puzzled. "Get it, moo-dur? Like a cow? And a mother? Only moo-dur?"

The light clicked on instantly, illuminating only a roll of her eyes before she grabbed me by the hand and turned to lead me down the hall to her cow. I guess it wasn't that funny.

At the end of the hall, light streamed in through the stairwell windows. She proudly pointed me to a large blob of color on a generous piece of salmon-colored paper on the wall. It was hard to tell where the grass ended and the cow began. Or where the sky began and the cow ended. It was colorful. It was beautiful. It was Sam.

"I love this, sweetie! You're such a good artist. I have the perfect place for this in my office."

I stroked Samantha's baby-fine hair as we admired her work together. She beamed and pressed her body against my left side, leaning into me. I kept my hand on her head and breathed in deeply, thanking God and asking Him to keep her safe, to give her this sense of safety and peace as long and as often as possible.

Purposeful heels made their way toward us. I straightened up, dropping my hand to Sam's back, and turned us both around. She held my hand again, and we walked back down the hallway to the line of her classmates. We let go of each other's hands, and I bent down to kiss her. She hugged me quickly and then turned and skipped before remembering to walk the last few feet to be the last in line. She nodded up at Sister Angela and then turned to smile and wave at me. I watched until she rounded the corner of the staircase, heading toward the after-school activities room on the second floor.

Hitting the waning light outside reminded me I was done for the day. But there was one more person my heart yearned to see today.

I gave my friend Gino Rivera a call. Thirty minutes later, I stood in a crowded Mexican restaurant, teeming with life on the city's north side, scanning the room for my swarthy friend. I noticed a colorful interruption in the dark sea of dress uniforms and business suits. Gino had taken up residence in a back corner booth.

When he stood to wave me over, his holstered gun was apparent on his right hip, nicely balanced by the large trucker's wallet in his back left pocket, silver chain linking it neatly to a belt loop in the front. He stood there waiting for me, his broad grin displaying perfect, white teeth, and I couldn't help but laugh out loud as I made my way over to him.

"*Mama mia!* You look good enough to eat, *m'hija*. I should look half so good as you do." Gino wrapped me up in his huge, bare arms, his tasteful, citrus scent enveloping me.

"It's so good to see you. I needed a Gino hug." I pulled back from him, straightening my jacket and repositioning my purse.

Gino was a man of many talents. People often underestimated him because they couldn't look past his do-rag and trucker's wallet. Inside his shaggy, affable Cuban head was a mastermind at work. He was always creating new criminal restraints, honing his private, patented collection of "catch-and-release accessories," as he referred to them. He split his genius into equal parts, also devoting a ton of time and energy to making big money by marketing his wares. He was adept at both ends of the business. He was also very good at reading my mind and calming my emotions.

"Now sit. Tell me everything. Especially all that I can do for the woman with the biggest heart in the universe." The warmth in his voice pulled me in.

His caring heart was just what the doctor ordered, and I relaxed with each word we exchanged. He drank Coke, but I opted for a frosty mug of dark beer. After giving him the thumbnail version of my misery over the first two beers, we ordered dinner, and I slugged down two more beers. I grew maudlin and moved into murkier territory, eventually working in tomorrow's looming visit with Maya.

"*M'hija,* don't you think you've had enough to drink?"

"Not yet." I took another sip and wiped the foam from my mouth before asking, "What keeps a life from unraveling, Gino?"

Silent, he considered my question for what seemed like an eternity. I drained the last drop of my stout Mexican beer while I waited.

"*M'hija*, this life is a gift, even on the most cursed of days. Even today, when you find yourself alone, you may meet the One who is most powerful in your weakness. You will know one day that what I say is true. Today is a gift, and every minute of this day has a purpose hidden in it for you. You can live each day, embracing your life."

Well, that had been worth the wait. Although, halfway into his second sentence, my head had started swimming. I vowed to switch to root beer next.

"But there's nothing left for me. Everywhere I turn, I'm lost. I know how to live at work, but I don't know how to live with an empty house. I've got nothing left. How do I live from the moment I get home to the moment I crawl back to work? It's like my life has turned into one long stint of solitary confinement. I can't stand the thought of living the rest of my life like this."

"But how can you think you are alone when Gino is right here next to you, plying you with free nachos? When all around you are people who love you? What about Nick? He's your good friend, no? What is it that compels you to spend your time in darkness rather than walking with me, with God, in the light? I can see you are in a lot of pain, but I'm here to tell you there is more for you, Josephine. God has a life of power and glory and unending love waiting for you to accept from His outstretched hand."

He stopped abruptly as I rolled my eyes at him. The beer was losing its effect on me.

"Please, not tonight. I don't want to hear the God-thing tonight."

Gino had lived a lot of life, and I felt bad whining to him and then shutting him down like that, but the last thing I wanted to hear right now was a bunch of religious mumbo-jumbo.

"Come to church with me, *m'hija*. He will prove himself to you."

"I don't think so, Gino, but thanks for asking."

His eyes saddened. I looked down at the table and shoved back my chair.

He stood up and hugged me as I prepared to leave. "Come and see me when you need a friend. I'm always here for you." Then he pulled out his cell and called me a cab. "I am such a good friend that I won't let you drive home in your condition. No arguments, please."

"Thanks, Gino. I'll call you soon." I couldn't meet his eyes before I turned and walked out into the cold to wait for my ride.

CHAPTER 16

I heaved myself out of the taxi and stumbled to the house. When was the last time I'd taken a cab home from dinner in the city? How much had I drunk? Who was I becoming? More importantly, where were my house keys? My head spun like a tilt-a-whirl, making it hard to rifle through my pockets and purse in the dark.

Fiddling with the key, I swore like a longshoreman and fumbled with the doorknob as I unlocked the door. It was stuck. Finally, I twisted it in anger. The weight of my shoulder pushing against the hollow wood forced the issue. The door swung inward. A thick cloud of fury swirled about me, settling on my shoulders, weighing me down. Pinpricks of fear skittered over my arms as I peered into the darkness. My hand grabbed the holstered Glock, resting at the bottom of my bag. I wrenched it free, comforted by the home-sweet-home feel of my most trusted partner.

I nearly had to pull my unresponsive feet up with my hands to get them to move me from the foyer into the empty kitchen and great room area. I reached the barren room, breathing hard, looking over my shoulder. I took a deep breath and snapped on the light.

The room was alien to me.

Faint kick marks jumped out at me under a new coat of paint on the walls. I tensed, remembering. Maggie's restoration project included a green sofa from her basement staged in the middle of the room.

I sagged down into the folds of the old sofa. The presence I'd sensed in the foyer had followed me. I stood up and tested my uneasiness by taking several steps in and out of the room. A palpable evil shadow stuck close to me, tracking me like some cosmic bloodhound. Or was it the alcohol? I took several deep breaths to clear my head while I loaded a full magazine into the Glock and chambered a round.

I pulled out my iPhone. There was no one to call, so instead I thumbed through my favorite pictures featuring me and the man I thought I knew. Melancholy memories flooded me, chased by longing and regret. Why did everything change after Del and I got married? Why had I put up with his abuse for so many years? I wanted someone to love and cherish me. But it wasn't Del. It had never been Del. I knew that now.

The raging presence beside me seemed to soften as my sorrow grew, inviting me to lean into it, to find my comfort in its murky shadow. I sank deeper into the sofa, and the darkness wrapped around me like a shroud.

I wept.

Del had chosen someone else. Rage grew inside of me. Animal sounds growled in my throat. I thought of him being happier without me. Worse yet, happier with someone else. How long had he been cheating on me? My eyes latched onto the honeymoon picture—the handsome, dimpled face of the man I thought I'd known so well. He'd left haunting memories and a thousand broken promises in his wake. The crushing existence of his new girlfriend mocked me.

The dark presence pulled at me. I still held the Glock in my right hand, and I pointed it up, admiring its sleek lines. The gun was one of the few standbys I could still call my own, and I respected the solid bond between us. At least the cold steel had not abandoned me.

The shadow offered me glimpses of my lonely, new world—disturbing images of myself embittered, friendless, and alone. It offered me two choices: succumb to the darkness and live in subjection to an obscenely evil presence, or continue to resist it. The notion of resistance felt like being battered by gale-force winds while carrying an impossibly heavy load down a rickety dock toward an ocean-liner-shaped mirage. Heading out to unknown seas.

A craving bubbled up from deep within me—steely and insistent. If this was my new life, I didn't want it. I wouldn't choose it. Not for another fifty years. Not for another fifty minutes. Death beckoned like a soft bed, and I sat there, silent and still, wondering what I would do next.

I pictured a blissful release and the quiet pleasure that would be mine if only I allowed my Glock's barrel to nestle against the roof of my mouth. The dark being wrapped itself around me. I welcomed its warmth.

I slipped the safety off and peered into the chamber of my Glock, relishing the sound and smell of it. The silvery-copper bullet lay there, eager and open-hearted, waiting for my command. I raised the stout barrel and rested it on my chin, squeezing my eyes shut. Was there a glimmer of hope anywhere within? One good reason to live, just one, and I'd be okay for another day. The dark presence growled beside me, urging me to pull the trigger.

Sam's sunlit figure appeared in my mind's eye. She was holding Nick's hand. Both of them glowed with a nuclear joy, and warmth flooded my heart. Stone shields slammed down like a theater curtain, filling my mind with tawdry visions of Del and his new woman, drowning out hope, extinguishing any remaining sparks of joy. Demonic shadows clung to both figures. My gut sloshed coldly. Goosebumps ran up and down my arms. The rank odor of rotten eggs assaulted my nose, mouth, and lungs.

You're not wanted here. You'd be better off dead. You hate it here. You're miserable. Come to me, and I will give you rest. Just one little sting is all you'll feel. Come on, you can do this.

My breathing stopped as I obediently opened my mouth just wide enough to welcome the Glock home. I smelled the metallic promise of the barrel as it rose to my lips, and I paused just before going all the way. The grotesqueries swirled on. I put my left hand over my eyes and shut them tight, Glock poised and ready in my right.

A shimmering image broke through my mind's black haze. A majestic, white horse thundered toward me—galloping, throwing its handsome head up into the clear-blue sky behind him. He whinnied at me.

Hope emerged, eclipsing my pain.

I leaned into the vision as the powerful animal pounded closer. He extended his long, beautiful neck to me in greeting, nostrils flaring. I could almost feel his warm, sweet breath, caressing my face.

What was I doing? I withdrew the Glock and released the magazine into my hand in one proficient motion. I pushed myself away from the dark presence and rose to my feet. The brilliance of the moonlight through the kitchen window melted away my anxiety.

I stood and secured my Glock in the gun safe. With an urge

to go riding, I marched into my hall closet for my hunt boots and riding pants, then threw them into the back of my car in the garage. I'd have time to hit the barn tomorrow after my mandatory stint with Maya.

I should've gone to church with Gino tonight. Two powerful forces warred within me, shoving aside anything I knew about grace and victory. Yes, I should've gone to church tonight.

CHAPTER 17

"You have such beautiful skin." Heat rolled up my sternum to my throat. Five long minutes of small talk with Maya, the shrink, had brought me to that pathetic statement. Did it sound as weird to her as it did in my head?

The two large mugs of coffee I'd poured down my gullet earlier this morning to compensate for my beer fest last night weren't helping. Tension snaked its way up my neck and dug into my forehead. Both temples pounded, and nausea roiled in the pit of my stomach. My forehead felt like a lighthouse, blaring through the night, drumming out my secret over and over. *Del left me! Del left me! Del left me for another woman!*

I sat stone still on Maya's sleek, leather couch, wondering if she could see the truth shining through the surface of my anger. I hated small talk.

"Thank you. If only it were half as beautiful as yours, I wouldn't think of bothering with these silly creams and such." Her faux, warm laughter was followed by the slightest shrug of her shoulders and a perfectly timed, breathless sigh. "Alas, I treat myself to only the finest moisturizers, and that, twice a day. Who're we kidding? Just between us girls—three times a day most days. But don't tell my therapist."

She leaned forward and issued a conspiratorial wink. I didn't like her vibe today. She seemed off. Most days I didn't like it, and I didn't like her. But hey, I had issues, so I let it slide, figuring it was yet another manifestation of my well-developed denial system working overtime. She seemed odder than usual today though, even for her. I didn't think I could blame it on my hangover. She kept turning a small, round jar in her right hand, as if the green glass housed a mysterious power.

She noticed me staring and lightly tossed it from hand to hand. She turned her attention from the jar to me. Was she angry? Glad to see me? I couldn't tell. "I'd offer you some, but it would be completely wasted on you and an insult to boot. Your beauty is equaled only by your valor. Now which is it that brings you here today?"

She switched back and forth from psycho, to best friend, to grandmotherly therapist at lightning speed. Trying to catch me off guard? Trigger some response? Who knew? I wasn't even sure why I was there myself. Maybe that was the point.

"Yeah, well, you got a call, didn't you?"

She smiled, crossed her legs, reached for her iPad, and sat back in her chair, all in one smooth motion. Her skirt rode up well past her knees, and I found myself comparing my own shaky demeanor to her polished confidence. I was definitely going to reward myself with some very fine chocolate once this mandated visit was over. Maybe some red wine to go with it.

"Jo, Jo, Jo, what *are* we going to do with you? Your humility amuses and impresses. But come now, we must have some feelings to discuss together today, do we not?"

This was going from uncomfortable to weird. She was teasing me. I just wanted to be done—to go home, watch a movie, eat some chocolate. Ride my horse.

"Well, first off, I hate him."

"Mmm, go on." Her smile had grown Cheshire-like.

"Aren't you going to write this down?"

"Now, Jo, you know I never forget a thing you say. Do go on."

"What can I say? You know the story. I really don't want to tell it again. I did my job. I was a pretty good wife. Del cheated—found somebody else. And I'd be lying to say I don't hate him. Shoot, I hate myself. And I'm so angry, I could kill him, kill them both with my bare hands."

"What about his friend? Do you want to kill her with your bare hands too? Why don't we start there?" She smiled, clearly enjoying this. She was evil.

A wave of darkness came over me, jumbling my thoughts. The pounding in my temples worsened, and I got so dizzy I thought I might fall over. Horrible pictures from my marriage and from the Little Sister Serial Killer crime scenes merged in my mind. I tried to edge away from the terrible bits and pieces of pictures floating around me, but I could barely move—like I was trying to walk through a force field of cosmic molasses.

As the dark consumed me, bone-deep, razor-sharp fear gripped me, but at the moment the unseen darkness overpowered me, a light space opened up in the far reaches of my mind. A deep peace spread through me, relaxing my body, freeing my mind, and calming my spirit.

Strong, clear words bubbled up from nowhere. *I know my sheep, and my sheep know me.* A sweet peace fell upon me as quickly as the darkness had. I stared at the movie screen in my mind's eye as another set of crystal-clear words took shape. *You are from God, little children, and have overcome them; because greater is He who is in you than he who is in the world.*

The dark pictures faded away, replaced by a sweet-smelling field of prairie flowers in a sunny valley housed between lush mountains on a beautiful day. A magnificent being stepped out from behind one of the mountains and revealed Himself to me. Somehow I knew it was God. He was glorious and beautiful beyond description. In His arms, He tenderly carried a little girl. He held her as if she were His only child.

It was me in His arms—a little girl version of me.

He wrapped His strong arms around my little-girl self, overwhelming me with feelings of warmth and safety, peace and power. I closed my eyes for a moment, leaning into His pure warmth. A strength I didn't know I had grew from deep within me. I smiled, bowed down, and opened my eyes.

Whatever had just gone on in my head, I didn't understand. My strength returned. My deepest sense of self—my balance, hope, and peace—was restored. The presence and the power of God sat next to me on the sofa. His Spirit was so real, I could almost touch Him. His light warmed me, rocking me to the depths of my soul.

Where once there had been darkness and pain, now there was peace. And through the warmth came the same message I'd seen in my vision. *Greater is He who is in you than he who is in the world.*

I didn't know where those words came from, or how long that vision had played out in my head. Was it a moment? An hour? A day? Had Maya seen it too? But with them, my confusion disappeared. I knew why I was there and how I would answer her questions about my mental health so that I could get clearance to return to work. I kept my head down in a show of false humility, allowing her to continue to assert authority over me. She'd been silent during my inner turmoil. What was she thinking?

It was time to put an exit plan in motion. "Maya, my marriage was bad. Del was and is an abusive jerk. I didn't deserve what he did to me. I can't change what happened, but I'll survive this." I took a deep breath to calm myself. "And Del? I haven't even begun to think about him. I'm devastated. I'm overwhelmed. But I'll get through this. I'm not alone. End of story. Now, why don't you sign this release, and let's call it a day."

She had me over a barrel, and she knew it. I couldn't return to duty without being formally evaluated. I braced myself for her next assault. I fully expected a fight, more of the twisted repartee she'd started this session with. Instead, there was more silence.

She sat back in her chair, eyes narrowed, appraising me. She held her Mont Blanc pen between her slender fingers. God nudged me, and I opened my purse, grabbed the fitness-for-duty form, and handed it to her. She never once looked at me as she signed, dated, and returned it.

I rose to my feet. God's warmth, His comfort, and His presence enveloped me. I couldn't wait to tell Gino about my encounter with what had to be the one true God. I turned, giving Maya an over-the-shoulder glance, as I walked out of her office without another word.

CHAPTER 18

I left Maya's office with an odd sense of peace, trimmed in what could only be described as joy. Not that happy Christmas morning kind of joy, but something more profound and far-reaching. I thought of it as a lingering aroma of God, and I longed to be back in His presence. Every part of my life seemed to be shifting and changing at such a rapid rate, even this new bundle of oppositional forces didn't surprise me. Who knew what would happen next? I just hoped He would be there to help me face whatever came next—whenever.

The station was a ghost town. I managed to dodge any meaningful human contact and hid out in my office until mid-afternoon, sorting holiday cards, reading reports, and surfing the federal databases in search of clues about the Little Sister Serial Killer. I was clicking open another file when my desk phone rang.

"Chief Oliver."

"Hey, Josie."

"Nick! Just the man I'm looking for."

"Well, I'm glad to hear that . . . *finally.*"

"Calm down, Tiger. I was just searching through VICAP for updates. You got anything?"

"No. He's remained dormant so far."

"Good. I hope we make it through the holidays this quiet. I've got enough horrors of my own."

"One woman's horror is another man's opportunity. When you coming home? You must've opened all your holiday greetings and moved your pens from one corner of your desk to another enough by now."

"Home? What do you mean by 'home' exactly?"

"Why don't you come on home and find out? I've decided to stick close to you for the foreseeable future. And you seem to have plenty of room right now, so I didn't think you'd mind if I rented out a spot in your basement."

"As in the one located underneath my house?"

He laughed. "Yes."

"Without even asking me or checking to make sure I have a renter's permit?"

"I bought groceries."

"Coffee?"

"Of course."

"Ice cream?"

"C'mon, beautiful. You won't even know I'm here. I'll be the model boarder. Besides, I'm off the clock until the end of the week. You should be too. See you in twenty."

He clicked off before I could object, and I sat alone for a moment, smiling at the thought of not having to face my empty life completely alone. I'd never really been a landlord before, but how hard could it be?

CHAPTER 19

"Hi, honey. I'm home!" I couldn't resist tossing the comfortable refrain to Nick as I walked through the door. Delicious Italian aromas lured me down the hall into the kitchen, and I wondered out loud if he might like to resign his current position and cook for me full time. You know, like Oprah's Bob Greene. I assured him his sauces alone would make it worth the effort.

He tossed me an apron from across the kitchen. "Baby, it'll take more than your sauce-whipped self flattering me to even make me *consider* working for you. But your love for all things Nick does give you an edge over the current competition. And being the mercenary I am, I'm perfectly willing to give you the opportunity to court me."

I stepped around the island as he finished his retort and hugged him hard enough to stop his talking for half a breath. The telltale key lay on the counter. Another mystery solved. Must've gotten it from Maggie. He kissed me on the forehead, gently pulling away as he looked me up and down and resumed his speech.

"But not in that outfit. Why don't you head upstairs and throw on some jeans while I finish up this sauce? I've got something I want to run by you when you come down."

"Okay."

I stood in the archway, watching him for a moment, overwhelmed with feelings of peace and joy and profound gratitude.

My solitary confinement had opened to let in a little light, offering me enough clarity to see that I was never alone. Even in those darkest moments, I'd been surrounded by the love of a God who sought me, even though I hated Him, hated myself. My heart swelled with gratitude. *Gratitude? Me? Where'd that come from?* I liked this new feeling. A lot.

It wasn't until I was halfway up the stairs that I sensed something was different. The stairwell had been repainted! And not only painted, but plastered. Each and every garish hole kicked or scratched into these walls not three days ago had been smoothed over and painted, erasing all evidence of my angry, exiting, soon-to-be-ex-husband.

At the top of the stairs, the woodwork looked all glossy and bright, and it hit me that Maggie and her merry band of carpenters even managed to touch up the baseboards all the way up the stairs and around this little landing. Even the door to my bedroom looked brand new. As I entered the room, I stopped to take it all in, hugging myself unconsciously.

The last time I stood there, the walls were ugly, bare, and broken—windows left open, curtains and shades ripped down, wall mountings half in and half out. Nick and Maggie had completely cleaned up the room. They must've hired carpet and window cleaners too. They'd had the walls and ceiling painted bright white, and one long windowless wall featured yellow wallpaper adorned with white roses, capped by a simple white wooden chair rail running from corner-to-corner. I felt like I'd walked into a new beginning.

Underneath a panel of windows that overlooked the small lake in front of my home sat a folded pair of worn and faded blue jeans. Maggie had chosen my all-time favorite brand of jeans in my size and laid them out on the freshly cleaned carpet underneath this sunny spot. She'd even washed them. An old FBI hoodie was sprawled out over a walnut chair in the corner of the windowed alcove. I kicked off my navy pumps, dropped my skirt to the floor, ditched my nylons, and grabbed the jeans off the floor. The soft, worn fabric caressed my thighs as I tugged the jeans into place by the belt loops and fastened the button fly. My feet sank into the plush carpet.

I took off my suit jacket and teased my silk blouse over my head, squirming happily into the fleece hoodie before walking back down to the kitchen. Nick turned and flashed a hundred-watt smile.

"You look great." He handed me a cup of strong, fresh coffee. "You're gonna live, sweetheart. I know it may not feel like it, but you're gonna live. Now drink up. I added cream and Splenda . . . just the way you like it."

"Nick, I. . ."

"Just relax. I'm here for you, and I'm going to do everything in my power to bring you out of this black hole and keep you safe."

"You shouldn't . . . you didn't have to . . ."

I was a blubbering idiot. Words failed me as I struggled to share my deepest gratitude with my best friend. Without success. All I could do was stand in front of him with my heart in my hands. He caressed my cheek and moved a strand of hair away from my face.

"It's what friends do for each other. It's nothing but a coat of paint, a couple of ounces of putty, and a few favors called in from some guys who owe me. There's much more to come over the next couple of weeks. Christmas came early. And nothing's free, babe. You know that. I already have a few ideas for a little *quid pro quo* when you feel up to tackling our case again. Plus, you haven't made me coffee in years."

He laughed, and mischief twinkled in his eyes.

"Yeah, right. Like you'd even *let* me make you coffee. You're impossible to please. I'd have to buy an espresso machine and make you one of those fancy drinks. And I'd never get the temperature and the foam just right."

"Oh, don't worry. I have much bigger plans for you than that, my friend."

"Do tell. And *please* make sure said plans involve some shopping on the side."

"Snap out of it. I got business on the brain. I got a special little project, and I think you can help me out like no one else can."

"What?"

"Ah . . ." He stepped closer. "You're just going to have to join me for dinner if you want to hear what I have in mind for you. And, by the way, you look amazing in your new jeans. Love your bare feet."

Nick launched into an opera song and pulled a smile out of me as I padded over to the counter. I drained my coffee and set the cup in the sink. He turned and offered me a delicate stemmed crystal glass of sparkling water.

"These aren't my glasses," I said.

"Housewarming gift . . . from me."

"Thanks. You have great taste in crystal." I smiled and took a sip.

"So, Buster's coming up for pre-trial."

"Buster?"

"Sure, Buster. You gotta get out more. Read a paper, watch the news. Take your mind off your own worries."

I stared at him.

He rolled his eyes as if talking to a fourth grader and continued. "Okay, let's review. Two weeks ago, a guy who calls himself Buster—real name's Cal Terry—became instantly famous during an evening homeowners' association meeting north of here. Ringing any bells?"

"Okay, yeah, but not all the details." A sick feeling gurgled in my stomach as the information materialized in my mind. I remembered it all right. I just didn't want to.

"Buster is the all-American dad who decided to reduce living expenses by whacking his entire family. Left 'em in the basement while he tried to figure out what to do with them. Long enough to get a fine from his HOA for foul odors. Ticked him off, so he decided to go to the next meeting of the association . . . armed."

"Right, I *do* remember. Turned out there was an off-duty cop on the board, noticed something strange about Buster from the get-go, and just happened to have his own piece on the ready, right?" I drank in the cool, lemony water, while Nick placed white dinner plates on the counter. I had forgotten the guy's name. "I just thought of him as Crazy Homeowner Guy." I added forks and knives to the place settings.

"Makes sense, given the media blitz. That's exactly how he was referred to at the time." Nick turned to inspect the pasta boiling on the stove.

"Didn't Terry go off somewhere during the meeting, and the dude jumped him?" I turned to open the fridge, searching for a refill.

"Yeah, but it was right up front, during the public comments portion of the meeting. And the off-duty cop was a woman. She gave him the eye, and he freaked, but she had her Glock out before he could take the safety off his .38."

I poured myself another glass of the soothing liquid. "And that was when everybody panicked and fled."

"Yep. One guy even jumped out a window, which was pathetic as it was right next to the door, and his wife, who he completely forgot all about, was left standing alone in the line of fire." He headed toward the sink, colander in hand.

"Oh, yeah. Then in the confusion, the off-duty cop shot the perp in the leg and cuffed him before he knew what hit him. What a piece of work that guy was. And what a shame about the psycho's family." I shook my head, trying not to picture the crime scene.

"That's Buster. Given that he was carrying a concealed weapon, they got a search warrant for other firearms, and that's when they found his family members in an advanced stage of decomp in the basement."

"Each one with a clean hole in the head. Twenty-two caliber, execution style. Some family man. Why the sudden interest in Terry?" I dug out some paper napkins from a bag on the counter.

"Well, the crime happened just about on the state line, and jurisdiction's been a battle ever since. His house was in Brown County, which is where the bodies were found, but the HOA's clubhouse is located in Wisconsin, which is where the takedown happened. So, Buster's got a court date coming up next week here in Brown County, and he needs an escort to the court-house. That's where you come in."

"Why me? I've got no interest or jurisdiction in this case. Besides, the FBI took over, and the evidence couldn't be clearer. So what's the deal? He into something bigger? What's in this for you? Or me for that matter?"

"This is still speculation, but a guy like him, he'd be a pretty good match for our unsub. He traveled a lot on his job. We can't prove it yet, but he looks real good for the Little Sister Serial Killer. And it coincides with the sudden silence on his end. You'd think he'd escalate for the holidays, and he hasn't."

The holidays? My face went white. I hadn't made the connection between our killer and the holiday season. Until now. A cream-colored envelope. An uneven, black scrawl. My first, middle, and last name—handwritten. A Christmas seal on the back. My stomach roiled, and a dull pounding started in my temples.

Nick stopped his meal prep and studied my face. "What is it?"

"I got an odd Christmas card a few weeks back at the station. I didn't think anything of it. I honestly just thought it was from some well-meaning village official and put it up with the rest of my cards. It's probably nothing."

"What's probably nothing?"

"Well, didn't the Little Sister Serial Killer send personal notes to his victims before making contact with them? And find a benign way to meet them before making the grab?"

"Yes." His eyes narrowed, and his body tensed as he leaned toward me.

"This may not be connected, but the more I think about it, the more it's giving me the chills. The note wasn't signed—not really."

"Was it signed with a letter, or an initial?"

"It didn't look like anything at the time. It just looked like, you know, a smudge or something. Never mind. Let's just drop it."

"Humor me, Josie. What did the note say?" He leaned back on the counter, arms folded.

"Something to the tune of 'Merry Christmas, Chief. Enjoy the holiday season.'"

"That's not ringing any alarm bells for me."

"That's not all. On the back of the card, he wrote a little New Year's inscription." The pounding in my temples was no longer dull. I grabbed my purse off the counter and rummaged around until I found a small bottle of aspirin. I poured three into my hand. "Give me a refill, would you, please? I'm getting the chills just thinking about it."

We both watched the clear liquid as he poured it from the sleek water bottle. He put the bottle down, handed my glass back to me, and looked at me so hard I turned my eyes away from his.

"What did it say?"

I gulped down the aspirin, remembering. "All the best in the New Year. Live each day like it might be your last."

"Where is it?"

"In my office." My breath came fast and shallow. I grabbed the counter edge to steady myself.

"That didn't strike you as odd until now?"

"No, I honestly kind of liked it. I thought it was from the Tim McGraw song when I read it. I didn't take it as a threat."

Nick's eyes were angry slits. His voice had taken on a dangerous tone. "Yeah. None of his vics did."

CHAPTER 20

My Christmas card admission had cast a somber note over our evening. In spite of the delicious food and all I had to be grateful for, I couldn't keep myself from veering down the Buster brick road. Nick was no better.

My nerves jumped into overdrive. "So, what now? What are you doing about this guy?"

"Take it easy. He's behind bars, remember? No threat there. My biggest worry with this case is on the evidence front. I spent an hour questioning him myself, and I'm telling you, I think he's good for it. I can *feel* it, but we can't prove it. Yet. We will though."

"Well, now I'm suddenly interested in your babysitting commission. It'll give me pleasure to get this sick psycho to the church on time."

"Oh, no. That deal's off."

"It most certainly is not! Now I care about this—a lot—and Gino will too. I guarantee you that." My voice rose an octave or two.

"We want to keep this one under wraps—ship and flip him over the holidays, fly under the media radar in case anyone connects the dots. I figured you could use the distraction of guarding the bus. But we need to rethink that now."

I didn't like his crisp tone. "What, now that the guy could be a real threat, you want a *real* cop on escort duty? Nice, Nick. Real nice."

"You know that's not what I meant."

"It's not like we'll be driving the bus. He'll be in cuffs and have like four armed guards on him in an armored vehicle, right?"

"Something like that."

"And if I know you, you've probably already lined up Gino to be my driver."

"Maybe."

"Which would mean I'd be getting a big night out on the town in Springfield on the state's dime, if I'm not mistaken. I'm guessing they'd want me for the tagalong transport first thing Saturday morning."

"You don't miss a trick, do you?"

"This job's a piece of cake. Why wouldn't I jump at it?"

"Oh, I don't know. Maybe because you're human, and you're not half as tough as you'd like the world to believe. This guy could be hard core. And you could be next on his list. I can't risk that. It's too close to home. You can sit this one out." Nick's voice resonated with concern.

"I've been sitting out way too much for way too long, and look where it's gotten me. What's the big deal? Gino and me, sitting in a van, trailing the big, bad, stupidly expensive, Illinois Department of Transportation super bus. What could be safer than being with Gino in a van over a holiday weekend? And besides, it's not like I've got any big plans at the moment."

"You got me there. I'm out of objections. But I will say this, if anything pops on this case, and this guy starts looking better as our serial killer, all bets are off. We'll start with sending your card to the lab. See if it starts singing."

"I can get behind that."

"All right then. Let's have some dessert and talk about something more pleasant—like your divorce."

CHAPTER 21

I spent the next few days out of the office, tending to my wounded pride, hanging with Jim, Maggie, and Nick and going back and forth from the gym to the local stable where I boarded my horse. By the time Friday rolled around, I was more than ready for a change of scenery.

Nick propped me up with strong coffee and visions of spending a day with Gino, and I got on the road before 6:00 a.m., hoping to beat rush hour on my way south. Hot coffee, talk radio, and two books on tape kept me company as I drove. After a while, the hypnotizing effect of the familiar drive took hold. Roadside markers rolled by in slow motion, relentless in the monotony of yet another trip down Highway 55. Mile after mile of flat, barren landscape napped on the side of the road, barely breaking into winter with the promise of slick roads wrapped in short, dark days.

I'd made the trip to Springfield so many times, I found it impossible to keep my mind on my driving. My drifting thoughts reviewed the events of the past week in vivid detail, frame by agonizing frame. Exhaustion crept in as the jagged scenes lingered in my mind's eye and endlessly dull scenery blurred past.

My eyelids grew heavy, and I caught myself nodding off for a second before deciding to take a little break, hitting buttons intermittently to haul the power windows up and down.

The chilly air revived me, and I caught the flash of a green-and-white road sign just in time to read the name of the sleepy, little bedroom community: Dellesville. *Not* where I was pulling off, no matter how tired I was, until the sign informed me it was another forty-eight miles between Dellesville and the next exit.

I really needed a break, but I decided a hair too late as the exit ramp appeared on my right like the last working elevator down from the top floor in a burning high-rise. I jerked the steering wheel to the right without letting up on the gas, semi-mindful of the cars and trucks behind me. My random act of kindness was met by electric hand waves, finger spelling, and horn honking as I careened up the ramp.

I came to an abrupt stop at the intersection. To my right was a strip mall. A full-service gas station boasting of diesel fuel, Wisconsin brats, and showers by the hour flanked the mini-mall. I turned left instead, drawn to the red-and-white awning of a decent fast-food restaurant. I was momentarily hypnotized by the hazy dream of a large turtle sundae with salted pecans.

I eased into a spot adjacent to the handicapped parking spot near the restaurant door. Marty Greene's name flashed up on my car monitor half a second before the phone rang. I answered it mid-ring.

"What's up, Marty?" Phone manners tended to evaporate the minute Samantha's social worker called.

"Hello, Jo. Everything's fine with Samantha, so please put your mind at ease." The tension in his voice belied his command to relax.

"But?" I prodded.

"But, there's something I just want to run by you." His baritone voice rose an octave.

"Go on." I straightened in my seat.

"Samantha's foster parents have noticed a woman in the neighborhood. She's not exactly menacing, but there's something off about her."

"Go on." My hand went involuntarily to check the Glock. It remained at the ready, tucked away in my shoulder harness.

"Evidently, this woman has been hanging around the playground in a park up the street. At first she said she was a nanny so no one thought twice about it . . . until Friday afternoon. Four of the five sets of parents who regularly see each other at the playground met at the same coffee shop and started comparing stories." Paper rustled quietly as he spoke as though he was reading his notes.

"And?" My brows furrowed hard enough to form permanent wrinkles on the spot.

"And the phrase, 'I thought she was theirs,' came out of all four couples when it was reported later. Along with, 'She seemed innocent enough.'" It sounded like he was tapping his pen against the desk. Marty was a retired cop. His do-unto-others core couldn't retire, so he turned to social work the day after he left the force. My hero.

"I still hear a 'but.' Why did the parents report her?" My spidey senses were on high alert.

"She was asking about Samantha. At least, we think she was asking about Samantha." He paused.

My heart stopped beating, and a cold stillness enveloped me. "She was asking *what* about Samantha? Did she use her actual name? Did she know who Sam was? How do you know it was Sam she was interested in?"

"We're not positive. She told two sets of neighbors she was a nanny for the Stevens family, one street over. She asked about the Christmas pageant. Said she loved the little donkey and thought she'd steal the show. But she also talked about the kids playing Mary and Joseph too. So it really could be any of them." His voice thinned out, and I struggled to hear him.

"So why the call?"

"Doesn't matter which one she was interested in, Chief. The Stevens don't have a nanny."

"That just rang the creepo-meter at seven bells." I gripped the steering wheel, my knuckles turning from pink to white.

"Yeah, I thought so too. The woman hasn't returned to the park either. Could be she's just a real pageant aficionado."

"Yeah. Could be."

"Could be just another one of your garden variety nut jobs too." Marty the cop was in full force.

"Could be."

"But, just in case, I did take the liberty of asking some old pals to run the descriptions I got of the mystery woman, but we hit nothing but brick walls and dead ends." Marty had been an excellent cop.

"So for now, we don't know what we don't know. And we live with the ambiguity. And pay for some off-duty pals to watch my little girl every time she leaves the house. Definitely during all rehearsals and performances of the pageant. At the very least." Since I couldn't be there, I wanted fierce warriors with modern weapons surrounding my girl at all times. I wanted the impossible. I wanted her to stay one hundred percent safe.

"I say we just hang tight and circle the wagons for now. Keeping an eye out is a good idea, but paying some off-duty cops to pack a little heat seems kinda—"

"Kinda like what you'd be doing if you were in my position?" Anger pushed its way up my back and into my throat.

"Maybe. Maybe it's a lot like what I'd be doing. Maybe it's overkill by two paranoid cops. I don't know. I just wanted you to know everything I know and now you do. A word of advice?"

"From you, Marty? Anytime, any place." I opened up my palms, flexing my fingers.

"I don't like the way this sounds any more than you do. But we've done all we can, and now that I've flattened you with all the bad news, here's some great news. Samantha's currently with her foster family on a skiing vacation far, far from here. And you and me and Mitch are the only ones having this conversation. So you've got some room to take a breath. Take a little break from all this stuff you've had piling up on those shoulders of yours and live a little." Marty had made the switch from cop back to social worker in less than sixty seconds.

"All right, Marty, I hear you."

"Please take care of yourself in the middle of this mess. You know the score—deep breaths, good thoughts, and the occasional ice-cream sundae. Whatever it takes to stay relaxed in the midst of the storms of life, right?" His words calmed me down like a warm hug.

I looked up at the front of the fast-food place where I'd parked and smiled. "Marty, I'm going to take this as a sign from God. I'm staring at a poster of ice-cream cones."

He laughed. "Well, then, go with God, Chief. I think my work is done here."

"I think so too. Thanks, Marty. I'll be in touch."

When I slid out of the car, my reflection in the full-length windows surprised me for a second. I'd nearly forgotten I was driving my squad car and was on a mission for the state. Dress blues were a requirement for state events, and I'd worn mine for the trip down.

I thought I cut quite a striking figure as I shut the car door, even with bloodshot eyes. A middle-aged couple beat me to the door just as I walked up the ramp, and the man held the door open for both his wife and me.

"Women and officers first," he said as he openly admired my Glock. "Nice piece there, ma'am."

The wife jabbed an elbow into her husband's thick waist as he whistled his approval, rolling her eyes at him and offering an apology to me all at once.

I smiled without breaking my gait. "Thanks. Came with the jacket."

I stepped past them into another line in time to quickly order an extra-large turtle sundae with a large, Diet Coke chaser. I strode to one of the small plastic tables, stiff muscles protesting with each step. I rarely wore my shoulder holster. Besides being too warm under jackets—to the point of ruining some of my favorite silk blouses—it rubbed against my ribcage, sometimes making me sore for days. Who knew what I was thinking earlier this morning when I put the whole package together. That was just it. I wasn't thinking. I was living moment-to-moment, and it was rubbing me raw in ways I'd never experienced before.

Another uncomfortable spot in my jacket erupted as I waited for my sundae, and I snagged a rolled-up *O Magazine* out of an inside pocket. I'd jammed this month's edition into my jacket on my way out of the house this morning, fully intending to unroll it and stick it into one of the longer, zippered compartments of my briefcase as soon as I got into the car . . . almost three hours ago.

I placed the magazine on the tabletop and smoothed it out, already looking forward to relaxing while reading its glossy pages. An acne-laden, carrot-topped boy of about fifteen walked up to my table. I offered him my red-and-white number, and he stood before me trembling, the tray he held between his scrawny arms shaking. Poor kid. My cop uniform must have scared him.

I stuck the number on his tray and picked up my sundae. The gangly boy backed into his retreat before I removed my hand from his tray, all the while staring at my ribcage. I really should've locked my Glock in the trunk before hitting the road today.

It was legal for me to travel armed, but it certainly wasn't comfortable, and I was sick and tired of being uncomfortable. I shoveled the first of many giant spoonfuls of ice cream, chocolate sauce, and salted pecans into my mouth, drowning my sorrows.

Even though it was winter, the cold dessert brought a surprising amount of relief, and I browsed through Oprah's latest fashions and "Favorite Things." The extra endorphins flooding my brain eased the tension, making me hyper-aware of the sharp discomfort of the gun digging into my ribcage. Looking around the restaurant, I pulled the Glock out of my holster and placed it on the table between two of Oprah's Book of the Month pages. Sweet relief washed over me, and I finished my treat in companionable silence with my fellow patrons.

Could have been they weren't used to seeing women eating ice cream for breakfast.

CHAPTER 22

The last leg of my journey to Springfield flew by. I listened to *The Best of Queen* full blast, punctuated occasionally by a Journey CD all the way to The Royal Plaza.

The whole day fell in line with my early morning start. Gino's smile floated before my eyes like a prize 4-H photo. We hadn't really talked since our rather chilly-ending dinner, and I was eager to clear the air between us. I was thrilled to see his van parked in the first row as I pulled into the hotel's expansive lot. He was out of the car before I even had mine in park next to his. His broad smile felt like home, and he shook his head and deepened his smile as I drew near enough for a quick hug.

"Hey, G! I *thought* I'd be riding with you on this crummy job." I pulled back from him, straightening my jacket and repositioning my briefcase strap on my shoulder.

"Crummy? This no is crummy job, *m'hija*. This is a dream job. Traveling behind a beautiful coach—fully armored and fully loaded—with you at my side. Carrying a pig's pig to a destination he does not wish to see. What could be better than this?"

"The bus one of yours, then?"

"*M'hija,* they are mostly *all* mine in this state. And in the next two states."

In addition to designing handcuffs, zip ties, and most other criminal restraint items my own station stocked, Gino's design talents bled over into vehicles and security systems. His was a dual talent in that his spin was often as potent as his designs. His products were in high demand before they left the drawing board. The armored bus transporting Cal Terry was one of his latest designs, and I was eager to see it rolling down the highway, sporting its first, dangerous, yet well-contained, criminal.

"Our ride is parked just outside the capitol building. I go to bring it up for us, and you will meet me in front of the steps." Gino's vibrancy eclipsed his free-style grammar.

"C'mon, cut me some slack, G. How about we meet a block up in front of the coffee shop?"

"Can I not entice you with an organic smoothie instead? As I have so often stated, you and coffee have become overly entwined."

"Coffee would be lovely. How about we meet in front of our little shop in twenty minutes or so?" Triumphant for the moment, I turned on my heel and walked off before he could object again.

He beat me to the coffee shop and stood up when he spied me from his perch on a stool at the counter. Two large paper cups and two paper bags were stuffed into a cardboard carrier, waiting on the counter. We walked to the new white van parked in front of the shop, meeting at the passenger door.

"Here *m'hija, favor de tomar* these mochas for me just a minute."

I took the tray from him, careful not to spill a drop from either cup. The new car smell imprinted into the vinyl seats made the perfect backdrop for the unique sights and sounds of the stark, white, panel truck. This simple vehicle, like the armored bus we would soon be following, came from Gino's private stock.

Gino was singing some lively Cuban tune as he sprinted ahead with the van, dedicating the next five minutes to catching up to an expensive, Buster-toting, Illinois Department of

Corrections convoy. He exchanged nods with the driver of yet another one of his vans as the first driver slowed down to allow us to slip into position behind the armored bus. He worked the accelerator for a while, jumping us ahead in fits and starts, until he found a pace he liked. He then settled back, turned up the music, and drove quietly for the first hundred miles while I dozed beside him.

Loud buzzing and humming noises came from somewhere deep inside the engine of the van as we drove through the barren land, rarely straying more than six car-lengths behind the behemoth before us. I'd never seen a bigger bus, and it looked to be brand new. Cameras were mounted along the top of the coach, and there were no windows, making its white sides seem unusually thick, even from this distance. Where did Gino get his ideas? It was all I could do to keep up with the maintenance needs of our vehicles. I couldn't imagine designing one.

In direct contrast to Gino's brilliance was the extreme lack of creativity apparent in the large, block letters announcing the owner of the monstrosity. ILLINOIS DEPARTMENT OF CORREC-TIONS was stenciled in large, black letters on both sides of the bus, and the letters IDOC graced the back panel . . . just in case you missed the sides, I guess. I couldn't help breaking our comfortable silence to ask him how much money he made on each bus.

"Forget the bus and the money, *m'hija*. Today we must speak of the unspeakable. I must hear from you about what you have experienced with that terrible man you married against my will."

So that was how this was going down. I sighed and considered clamming up for the rest of the way, but thought again. "Well, Gino, it's . . . complicated. I . . ." I turned my head away to study the desolate landscape, flashing by outside my window. "I don't have it in me today." I tried to stem the tide of his need to know, but the dam had already broken.

"*M'hija*, you got it all. God has crafted a masterpiece. You are fearfully and wonderfully made in every way. And you got the brains, no? Not to mention beauty as well. Your talent surpasses that of most men—those who are not so talented as me, *verdad*?"

"Yes, well, maybe, but Gino—"

"You know your way around guns, knives, kitchens. You are every man's dream wife. What could that horrible man be thinking? It makes no sense. But still, I am glad you are free of him. It will be for the best. You will see. Our great and merciful God has something so very much better for you."

My only answer was more tears. So far, our little chat was not going according to plan.

"Is okay, *m'hija*, you can cry to me. You need to maybe get it out of your system."

"Where do I even begin? It's a sad story. And I hate it, and I'm ashamed of it, and I wish it weren't mine, but it is." I sniffed and angrily wiped a tear from the edge of my eye. "He abused me, Gino. Del is an abuser. He hit me. He did things—nasty things. It nearly killed me, but it didn't. I shouldn't have stayed, but I did, and I wish I hadn't. I guess I wasn't brave enough to leave. So now I'm reaching down deep inside to gather all the courage I can find just to get through the day. That's all I can do right now."

"That's all any of us can do. We only have today. You have to keep reaching for your strength within, *m'hija*. And as you reach, our great and merciful God is reaching for you. You just don't know it yet." He paused and looked over at me. "I am not loving this new you so much. I want my feisty Chief Josie to come back. I want you to remember you are a daughter of the King of Kings."

Del's face floated before me, and for a moment my heart opened just a crack. Unbidden pictures of God assaulted me, and my heart turned stony. Anger rushed at me from within, and I raised my voice, clenching my teeth as I spoke.

"I *know* I've got it going on. I know you'll never understand this, but I lost it for a moment—lost sight of who I am for a season. A really long and terrible season. I got hooked up with Del, and before I knew what hit me, I lost myself completely."

"Come back, *m'hija*. It is time. God calls you gently to Him."

Gino's words reminded me of a hummingbird. I'd like to know them, to let them in, but there was no place for them to rest. Gino's kind of calm never seemed to find me. Maybe I'd been keeping too many secrets from too many people for too long. Maybe today I'd start to let the secrets out. One little humming-bird secret at a time.

"On our honeymoon, Del was wonderful. He was thoughtful and charming. He reeled me in by being the man every woman's looking for."

"The wounds are deep, *m'hija*. But the healing will be deeper."

"The first time he hit me, I was stunned. And I never told anyone. I couldn't." I took off my gloves and stared at them resting on my lap. "We were driving home to Illinois from my family's home in Wisconsin. He was at the wheel. After the honeymoon . . . maybe three or four weeks later. He seemed to be angry all the time, simmering like an over-cooked stew. I thought it was me."

"So much pain. So many lies he had you believe. And you— you are the sweetest and the toughest, and well, let's face it, you can also be just a little bit frightening, but—"

"I was so confused. It never happened in a straight line. He would hit me, or push me, or threaten me, and as quick as the episode began, it would end, as if it never happened. In the beginning, I would press him about why he acted that way, and he would cry. He'd beg for my forgiveness and promise never to do it again. Then it would stop . . . for a while."

"But nothing ever really changed."

"No, nothing changed."

"You should've put a bullet in his head right up front, *m'hija.* Did you not, at the very least, think of it?"

"I couldn't. Every time I thought about standing up to him, I just fell back into myself. I froze—couldn't move, couldn't react, couldn't bring myself to leave him like I should've done a thousand different times. I second-guessed my every move."

"It is so hard to believe. When are *you* unsure of yourself? You are the wisest, strongest lady I know. This is a side of you no one else has perhaps seen—a side that motherless son of a rat did not deserve! This tender Jo is to be cherished, and this . . . this *puerco malisismo* should have been adoring you, protecting you. Not . . ." He shook his head. His dark-brown knuckles grew lighter as he gripped the wheel so hard I wondered if it would snap in two.

"Gino, I'm okay."

"No, listen to me. A man must never hit a woman, no matter how much she annoys him. Never! Your husband is a coward."

Opening his hands wide, Gino drove as if making supplication on my behalf. Dreary, roadside scenery zipped past the windows as he spoke. "You have made me sad this day with your story. Happy to have you tell it to me, but sad to hear it. Sad as you had maybe forgotten that you had so many friends. You could have come to me or to Nick. We would have helped you. And let us not forget, *m'hija,* you have a gun."

"Seems like all I've got sometimes is my fear and my doubts and my shaky second-guessing, but yes, I most definitely still have you, Nick, Mitch, Jim, and Maggie on my side. And I need you. I need you all."

Gino's cell phone chirped, but he ignored the text and glanced at me. I looked out the window as a BP station flitted by on my right.

"But why, *m'hija*? Why could you not stand up for yourself? Fight back? Leave?"

"I don't know. I just couldn't. I just kept caving in."

"Okay, this I can accept. But then, why did *he* decide to go? What happened to make him cheat on such a beautiful wife as you?"

I squirmed in the seat, hungry all of a sudden. A large bag of barbeque corn nuts would be welcome right about now. "That's the wrong question at this point, G. I know why he left me. He made that pretty clear. The real question is, how much is he going to hurt me on the way out?"

CHAPTER 23

"Sí, senor. . . Uh-huh, uh-huh . . . What? Really? . . . Humph. Yes. I will." As soon as he ended the call, Gino turned to look at me for a few seconds. Something was definitely not okay.

"This day may have just gone to the dogs, *m'hija*."

"What?" Sometimes even I couldn't make heads or tails out of my friend's colloquialisms.

"We maybe have some problems coming to us very soon. Here." He handed me his phone. "Call Jaime. I need to find out what exactly is going on up there."

"Why? What did they say—?"

"Just do it, *m'hija*. We got some engine trouble. Maybe gonna have to pull off, maybe even head back."

"G, you never pull out of a convoy—"

"*Sí, m'hija*, I know this. Now please, call Jaime for me."

The tone of his too-quiet voice propelled me to stop talking and make the call. The guard in the heavily armored bus in front of us answered before the end of the first ring. I stuck the phone into Gino's hand, but I could still hear every word Jaime said to him.

"We've got state troopers coming in from three sides. Closest unit is two, maybe three minutes away. Donnie, in the lead van, wants us to take an exit about six miles from here. Says he'll have a trooper clearing it before we get there, and he's got two more

units hugging the highway on either side of the station already."
Gino curled his lip as he listened to Jaime's metallic voice.

"Two more single squads are coming from another county
over. There's a full-service truck stop at the exit. Supposed to have
a couple of grease monkey, gear-head types practically living
there. Thinks they might be able to help us out. Fast service too."

"What? Native getting restless perhaps, Jaime?" Gino's voice
had morphed into a snarl.

If Jaime caught the warning, he didn't heed it. He was bound
and determined to take a quick mechanic break. He was leading
us into dangerous territory.

"There's only a few of us know enough to be really worried
about him, if he is who we *think* he is," Jaime said. "Other two
guards should probably be worried about him too, and would
be if they knew. Donnie says to keep him shackled, keep the
bars up, doors sealed. This won't be a potty break. Donnie's
boys are joining me in the bus, and we'll keep machine guns
trained on him the whole stop, just in case he decides to get
stupid on us."

"That stuff don't happen, *amigo*. That's just Donnie being
Donnie. You know he'd love to pop a convict any chance he got.
It is possible he perhaps busted up the bus himself just to have
such an opportunity as this. Yes. Of course. *Luego*."

Gino tossed the cell my way and pounded his palms on the
steering wheel, looking for all the world like a little boy on a big
wheel. "We're gonna have us some fun today, *m'hija!* Seems there
is some trouble with the bus."

Long, barren fields zoomed by the window. "Glad you're feeling so good about this. I'll just take a little catnap while you boys
work it out. I've seen enough of Buster's mug shots at the station

this week to last me the rest of my days. I don't even plan to get out of the van. You're flying solo, buddy."

"Oh, no. This is too much fun. We'll both be there, weapons drawn, hoping to get in some target practice. *Sí*?"

His accent grew thicker, and I swear his boyish excitement was contagious. The longest cargo train in history inched along beside us as we followed the bus.

"So, just in case, refresh my memory here. We stay *in* the van. Can't leave unless visibly provoked, or asked for backup. Or do we *leave* the van and can't return until there's an all clear? What's the latest protocol on this rock-and-roll highway bull?"

"Ha! You're getting lax on me, *m'hija*! Too many banquets, not enough—"

"Hey! Did you see that?"

"What?" He stared at the strip mall long and hard and then turned a reproachful gaze to me. "*M'hija*, you stay in the van! You got that? Me too. We don't leave for nothing. You leave only if—"

"One or both of is dying for a little road food and maybe a little caffeine, right? I mean, we're talking purely medicinal. Is that what you were about to say?"

"No, *m'hija*. We leave only to save someone . . . a good someone. We got a man down, we go out. Even for the ugly man. No man down, we stay right here."

"Okay, ease up on me already. I got it."

The upturned wrinkles around his eyes hinted at a smile from the secrecy of his reflector shades. I knew I was making some headway. I could almost taste the fresh bag of corn nuts.

"C'mon, we're barely breaking protocol today, G. Just for a minute. Two, tops. Humor me. It's almost Christmas."

"*M'hija! Estas loca!* We are staying put. I don't need a thing. And you hardly ever eat. Unless you are on the road. And then you eat like one possessed. This I have never understood."

My subtle sideways glance moved him, and the crack grew wider. I was in. Tears welled up, a slight sniffle escaped, and I looked right at him. The armored bus ahead of us veered onto the exit ramp behind the lead van. Both vehicles slowed to a stop, preparing to turn left onto the four-lane road that would lead to the service station. My eyes never left his face as he followed the lineup through each maneuver, and I didn't say a word. I didn't have to.

"*Santos, ayuda me!* Stop it, woman! Okay, all right! But be fast. I cover for you, but you better run, and you better beat the troopers and slide so quickly back here . . ."

I was out of the van and sprinting toward the strip mall before he could finish spitting out his final warning. Less than three minutes later, I launched myself back into the van, snacks in hand.

The first trooper pulled into the parking lot just as my door latched. Gino was chewing on a straw, hands ten and two on the steering wheel. He held up a finger and nodded his head at each trooper as they squealed in, surrounding the bus. He kept his eyes riveted on the vehicle ahead of us, playing it by the book.

"Lucky for you, I am a man who understands you, *m'hija*."

"Huh?"

"I can appreciate your needs." Gino's lips didn't move, nor did he look at me while signaling his colleagues with his finger as they crawled past us.

"You, my friend, are a Renaissance Man *par excellence*."

"And *you, m'hija*, are a very bold woman . . . with a little corn-nut issue."

"Gino, baby, all you gotta do is ask. I'll happily share."

His indignant snort and the hint of a sideways grin were my only answer. We sat and speculated about possible reasons for the breakdown for the next twenty minutes. As luck would have it, one of the two grease monkeys had been riding shotgun with one of the troopers. The men edged their vehicles around the bus as they pulled in, circling it like a school of sharks.

Once all units were present, Donnie opened the armored bus door and waved, signaling all who were interested to join him for the prisoner watch. Officers rolled out of their units, guns drawn, walking as fast as they could to get to the bus steps, like die-hard sports fans waiting to catch a loaded charter to a Brewers' game. Between all the members of the makeshift army, the armored bus was up, running, and back on the road in less than fifteen minutes.

Gino changed song lists as the Spirit moved him while I happily tore into a fresh bag of barbeque corn nuts. He snapped his fingers in the air and pointed at me.

"*La hija de m'hija*—how is she? Where is she for the holidays?"

I smiled and reached into my purse, rummaging until I found my stash. "How great is this?" I held in my hand a perfectly formed, plastic Holstein cow to add to Sam's collection. As far as collections went, her Holstein habit was an easy one to meet, especially since most truck stops in Illinois and Wisconsin stocked them.

"Ah! Now I understand your mad dash. You were, of course, only thinking of the child."

"Exactly." I shifted in the seat, putting the prize back in my purse. "It's hard to say. She's scrappy as ever, strong as ever, and is on her fourth foster home in nearly two years."

"Samantha should not have to deal with this. And she is all of what—three, four?"

"She just turned six this month. I'm still seeing her as often as the courts and the families will allow. You're invited to join me for the Christmas pageant at her church. She's really excited about playing a part this year."

He nodded, smiling. "This I will not miss."

I turned soft eyes toward him, ready to share my heart's desire. "I want to adopt her, Gino. And with Del out of my hair, I will. I'm already all about it. My attorney buddy is drafting paperwork and a game plan over the holidays for me."

He nodded his head as he drove. "There can be no greater gift, *m'hija*. For this child and for you. Uncle Gino approves."

"I had no doubt." Other doubts, yes. I'd never been a parent, much less a single parent, and I welcomed the opportunity to share my fears out loud. I spent the next two hours dissecting them with Gino, preparing to accept the gift of a six-year-old girl into my life.

CHAPTER 24

I fell asleep again for the last few minutes of the ride, waking up when the van slowed to a stop and the temperature shifted dramatically. Gino had opened the door for me. I did a quick cat stretch and squeezed the sleep out of my eyes.

"You are finally awake? Good! I can't hold this door open for you all night." Gino leaned over me to release my seat belt and help me out of the van.

"I must've dozed off for a minute there. Sorry. What are you doing? Where's the bus . . . and Buster?"

"I'm letting you out here at the front, *m'hija*. Like the perfect gentleman I am. No need for you to join me for another tour of the seedy side of Brown County to deposit this animal we're hauling."

"No, I'm going with you. Keep driving around to the back."

"Forget it. I got my orders. And anyway, isn't that your right-hand *mujer* coming around the corner with your ride home?"

I followed the nod of his head toward the approaching set of headlights, fully awake now that the chilly, night air washed over me. Sure enough, Mitch pulled into the parking spot in front of us as Gino remained double-parked in front of the courthouse steps. The IDOC bus had been surrounded by both the heavily armored county van and two county squad cars.

This was like the fourth of July for some of these guys. Not much happened in our little county during the holidays beyond the occasional domestic violence call. The deputies wanted to get up close and personal with a real criminal while they could. There were often "accidents" in transport, and they happened more often than not as guards escorted prisoners from cell to cell. From the looks of the headlights and the sounds of the voices gathering, there would likely be more than one "accident" for Buster to contend with tonight. He might've earned it in my book, but with Gino in the background, the other guys would be kept in line. He'd long ago proven his mettle as a local, county, and ultimately state cop. Respect as deep as his stayed alive among the boys.

"*Vaya, m'hija!* I gotta go see about keeping the integrity of our boys in blue intact."

"All right, all right. Go be the amazing man you are. But first, I get a hug. Thanks for the truth talk, Gino. You mean the world to me."

"*Vaya con Dios, m'hija.*"

I nodded and half hugged the rugged man before sliding out of the van. I leaned in to grab my purse before shutting the door and waving him away. He jogged back to the driver's side and jumped in. Flashing the lights, he drove off after the bus, a growing parade of squad cars falling in behind.

Mitch and I launched into the standard news and gossip from her day's shift as I drove her home. We pulled into her driveway for the drop-off without wasting a minute. We were both exhausted.

"Thanks for the company, Mitch. See you tomorrow. Say hi to your hubby for me."

I hugged her before giving her a gentle push toward her house. I watched her walk up the stairs and waited for her husband to come to the door. We exchanged happy waves as he ushered her in, and I pulled out of her driveway.

The front of my home was all lit up as I approached, and for a moment I froze, a terrifying sense of *déjà vu* falling in around me. The dread evaporated as I realized it was something really different.

The scene was enchanting. My house was framed in thousands of white holiday lights. The porch was lit so brightly I could see the fresh paint that livened up the wooden decking and the sparkling glass of the porch lanterns from the end of the driveway. Parking in the driveway, I spied white, icicle lights hanging from the eaves, a lit Christmas tree set up in front of the living room window, and decorations of varied shapes and sizes scattered along the length of the front porch. I got out of the car and walked to the front steps to get a closer look. Fragrant, green boughs curled around the square pilasters of the farmhouse porch and streamed down the railings.

At the top of the stairs, I nearly doubled over laughing. Shapely urns held a festive collection of plastic rifles, shotguns, and what looked like pink, plastic machine guns, each decorated with lively bows of every color, some with poinsettia flowers coming out of the business end. It was hilarious. It was beautiful and must've taken someone a great deal of time to pull together. I grabbed one of the longest plastic rifles with its protruding poinsettia, ran my hand down the length of the barrel, and burst out laughing again.

"Dude! What's so funny? Never seen a little Christmas display before?" Jim walked up the steps with Maggie by his side. I hugged them both, still laughing.

"Anybody can do a crèche. I figured you needed something a bit more *avant garde*." Jim's widespread arms gestured to his handiwork.

"Thank you! Maggie . . ."

"I had absolutely nothing to do with it. This was all Jim's idea."

"You guys . . . I . . . "

Maggie and I just stood there, grinning and crying on my front porch. Jim rolled his eyes and shooed us toward the front door.

Maggie smiled at me and reached into her pocket. "Oh, here. Take your house key back. I'm staying here with you two tonight. Think of me as a babysitter. For your virtue. You'll thank me later."

As I opened the front door, I saw an unshaven, wet-haired Nick, sauntering down the stairs. "Welcome home, Josie. Like the decorations?"

"They're stunning." I stepped into the living room and found myself momentarily speechless. I had only glimpsed the Christmas tree from outside, but now I could see the detail and care with which it had been set up.

A six-foot artificial spruce, completely decorated, stood in the corner between two of the front windows.

"You like?" Nick grinned from ear-to-ear.

"I like, Nick. Thanks. Maybe Christmas won't be such a bummer after all."

"Say, Jim," Nick said. "Could you tell me what day this is?"

"Sure, Nick, I'd be glad to. Why, it's Friday night."

"Friday night? Really? Hmm. Isn't there some sort of suburban ritual involving pizza on Friday nights?"

Jim nearly danced over to the double ovens recessed into the far wall of the kitchen and pulled open the doors simultaneously to reveal two, large, thin-crust pizzas.

"You guys! It's midnight. We can't be eating pizza like a bunch of teenagers at this time of night." I looked from one face to the other. Not a lick of support coming from this crowd.

"Or, *can* we?" Maggie chimed in, and I caught a quick wink from Nick.

Jim waved a slice of pizza under my nose, chasing out all vestiges of resolve, and the party began. We spent hours eating snacks and laughing deep into the early morning. We even put our coats on and shot a few frigid games of makeshift darts in the garage before the party broke up. By the time I collapsed on the sofa in the great room, my face was sore from smiling. The power of their friendship still surrounded me.

Nick had agreed to stay with Jim and Maggie in their comfortable guest room at the urging of all three of us. Designer sheets trumped the basement's sleeper sofa, so I was truly all alone in my big, empty house. It might've been my exhaustion, but in the early morning solitude, I felt as if I weren't alone, almost as if Gino's God was watching over me.

As I fell into bed upstairs, I held on to the warm feeling as long as I could, and as I drifted off to sleep, I realized I was actually looking forward to tomorrow.

CHAPTER 25

I awoke to an eerily quiet Saturday morning. Today marked the beginning of the third weekend after the unthinkable had happened, and I felt a solid sense of peace as I slowly came alive, limb-by-limb. This morning there was something more. I felt the presence of God so firmly that I half expected to see Him materialize before me. The thought came to me in a flash and then dissolved, but His peaceful presence stayed with me. Maybe I needed more sleep. Maybe I was hallucinating.

The airplane motor sounds of coffee beans grinding convinced me to get out of bed, toss on my new jeans and hoodie, and head downstairs for a little surveillance of my own. I'd programmed the coffeemaker before I went to bed, a small semblance of normal returning to my world. I'd even placed Nick's navy FBI coffee mug next to the machine, along with my requisite two packets of Splenda.

I'm home. Smiling at the idea, I opened the fridge, and the large carton of heavy whipping cream on the top shelf caught my eye. Nick's handwriting, on a note he'd taped to the carton before his departure last night, left me instructions to be careful and check the door locks twice.

I poured myself a cup of coffee, doctored it to perfection, and headed over to the comfy sofa. The saxophone sound of my phone rang softly inside my purse, and I rooted around in the bottom of it. Unfortunately, a cop was always on-duty. My grumbling turned to delight when I saw Georgi's name on the caller ID right before I hit the little green button.

"Hey, Georgi!"

"Hey, Jo! How are you, girl? How you holding up? Cliff and I are worried sick about you, and we really want to see you. What're you doin' today? You're not working, are you?"

"The day is all mine." I took a sip of coffee and almost purred like a cat.

"Great."

"Why? What's up?"

"You had breakfast yet?"

"Nope."

"Good. You dressed yet?"

"Yup."

"Perfect. You had your first cup of coffee yet?"

"I'm on it. I may even have two or three before I'm through."

"Pour it into a travel mug and get your lazy butt off that sofa. Cliff and I are taking you out to breakfast, so get moving. We're starving, and it'll take you forever to get here."

I could envision her triumphant smile as she hung up the phone without giving me time to reply. Looked like I was headed to Wisconsin.

Fifteen minutes later, I drove my SUV north, waiting for the heat to kick in as I shivered in the frigid morning air. I put my portable coffee mug down only long enough to find acceptable tunes on the radio. It was just past 6:00 a.m., and the drive time would easily be cut down by a third because of the early hour and the breezy feel of Saturday morning traffic.

Perfect day to cruise up north to see my people. I decided not to let family members know about this quick trip, knowing it'd take what little spare energy I had to fill Georgi and Cliff in on this new chapter of my life's story. I was not looking forward to that part of the visit, but at the same time, it'd be nice to get it over with.

Sparse traffic on I-94 North freed my thoughts to wander. Dark thoughts and significant doubts about Cal Terry as the Little Sister Serial Killer flitted through my mind as I drove. Then thoughts of Del floated out next to me. I pushed them as far to the back of the car as possible, but they crept right back into the front seat with me. One of the last times I had traveled this stretch of highway, Del had been with me.

CHAPTER 26

The window was barely open, letting in some of the frigid air. I drove over the Wisconsin state line shortly after 6:30 a.m., shaking my head to dislodge the bad memories of Del and our accident. I was on a new road now—safe, away from him, and heading toward my homeland. My memories drifted back to simple days spent riding horses, skipping school, and cruising the lake with my buds.

The night Georgi and I watched from the stands as Cliff made school history with the winning touchdown, clenching the conference title. That was the moment Georgi turned to me and swore she'd marry him one day. And I was by her side at the altar two years later when she did. Nineteen years old and right out of high school. I thought she was crazy, but I still stood beside her, both of us dressed in our finery, holding bouquets carefully crafted by one of her cousins. And now, years later, theirs was the happiest, strongest union around.

I slowed down to take the ramp to Highway 33 at a reasonable speed, turning right at the stop sign on autopilot. Passing through the Narrows between Baraboo and Portage, I enjoyed the stark beauty of the Baraboo Bluffs, flanking either side of the two-lane road. I'd spent many fine days horseback riding up and down those steep, rocky hills. Seeing spots I knew so well from the road brought me back to the center of my life, my world.

I looked forward to seeing the hundred-year-old Victorian frame house on Fourth Street that Georgi and Cliff had called home since their wedding day. They'd bought the house from Cliff's grandmother, and I remember at the time thinking it confining and old and horribly small townish. Now it seemed like paradise, and I was eager to see any new touches and additions they had created together.

Georgi's decorator eye teamed with Cliff's fine craftsmanship and attention to detail had transformed the little house into a highly sought-after retreat. They'd turned down offers over the years that could fund small countries. I was looking forward to seeing what Georgi might have done with it for the holidays.

Cliff was on the lookout as I parked on the street in front of their lovely home. He opened the front door as I climbed the first step of the front porch. A brass bugle nestled in fresh greenery adorned the front door. Georgi had also hung bugles of different sizes, artfully entwined in long-needled swags, along the porch railing and from the eaves on the low-slung roof. White lights ran the length of the garland, decked with large, red bows along with clusters of red berries between the bugles and bows. Cliff opened the door wider, and I could see Georgi hustling in the background, locking their two large labs in the kitchen and then grabbing two leather coats.

"Hey, Jo! You look amazing!" Georgi's hug melted me. We skipped down the stairs while Cliff locked the front door and trailed behind us toward my car.

"Nice ride. Can I drive?" Cliff zipped his coat and headed into the street toward the driver's side.

I laughed and tossed him the keys. Georgi headed toward the back, shaking her head and carping at her husband. I relaxed in the passenger seat, thoroughly enjoying Cliff's pleasure as he drove the few short blocks to The Good Eats Cafe. Bracing against the wind as we crossed the parking lot, we grabbed hands as we jumped over the curb and ran under the awning to the cafe door. We huddled inside the tiny vestibule behind a short line.

"Good grief, guys. I haven't been here for at least a hundred years. I can't believe how much this place has changed. It's so elegant now."

"New owners. Put all kinds of money into it. Probably losing a ton of money. Gotta have some pretty deep pockets is all I can figure." Cliff pulled off his gloves.

These were the sounds of my hometown. The place was packed. I smiled and looked around the room, studying the patrons. Most of them looked vaguely familiar.

Georgi brushed off the back of Cliff's jacket with one of her mittens. "You don't know that, Cliff. They might be doing just fine. In fact, I've heard they're way past breaking even. There's even talk of expanding. Might buy the store next door since the electric shop is gone. It's been on the market for nearly a year now."

We stood to the side of the counter next to a few other small groups waiting to be seated. A large man in a chef's apron appeared out of a swinging door on the right and motioned to the hostess who immediately seated us in the one empty booth, raising the ire of the others waiting in line before us. Cliff and the man in white nodded warmly to each other.

The waitress filled Cliff's cup with hot coffee and placed a small glass of orange juice in front of Georgi. I turned up my own coffee cup and smiled my thanks as she filled it.

"Good to see you again, Miss Jo."

I looked into her eyes. She was very familiar, but I wasn't coming up with a name. Vague images of a slender runner dashed through my mind's eye, bringing memories into view. I watched her dart off to the counter. "Georgi, who—"

"That's Timke's little sister."

"*That's* Timke's little sister? Boy, are we getting old. She was what, about five years behind us? I remember you babysitting her and us coming over to clean out the fridge every now and then."

"Yeah. And I got blamed!"

"You've made up for it nicely though, dear." Cliff gave her a sideways hug as he spoke, limiting her ability to slug him in the shoulder.

"Anyway, since when has this place gone all yuppie haven on us? What's with the brass railings and ferns?" I looked around at the nouveau décor, shaking my head.

"Hey. That may be true about the ferns and all, but you really have to give 'em credit for restoring the ceilings, floors, and wood trim in this place." Cliff snapped open his napkin, placing silverware on either side of his plate.

"Okay, I'll give you the ceilings. They're good looking, but who does tin ceilings? What am I, on an episode of *Antiques Roadshow*? I came here for a little breakfast and a lot of gossip. You're supposed to take my mind off my woes. One more line about the décor, and I'm going to *have* to talk about the Little Sister Serial Killer just to change the subject."

"Jo, please—" Georgi's voice rose at the mention of the case. She never understood how I could look at dead bodies and not faint. She couldn't even watch *CSI* on TV.

"Sorry." I opened up a creamer and doctored my coffee. There I went again, ruining a perfectly good morning. I needed to downshift into small talk. "Order the country skillet and a bottomless cup of coffee for me, Georgi, would you please? I'm going to go to the girls' room to splash some cold water on my face and then come back and start this conversation over."

I winked, slid out of the booth, and headed to the back. I was getting antsy. Maybe Nick had an update for me. I slid my phone out of my back pocket and sent him a quick text, ANY NEWS? before stepping into the bathroom.

I was examining my bangs when my phone buzzed. Less than ninety seconds. Not bad. My neck stiffened at his one-word response.

YES.

Oh, no, please don't let there be another one. It buzzed again while I was compiling a response.

YOU'RE BEAUTIFUL, AND I MISS YOU. HURRY HOME.

I blew out a belly full of air and shook my head, already texting my response.

IDIOT.

I hit SEND and rejoined my friends.

"So, did I miss anything?"

Apparently, I had. Their faces reddened, and they lurched into silence as I climbed in the booth and sat opposite them.

"What? Spit it out." I cupped my hands around my refilled mug and waited.

Cliff must've been the designated talker. "Jo, it ain't right. It just ain't right."

Georgi grasped my hand. "You know I've had your back all your life, and I'm riding with you through this storm too. I just wish there was something we could do for you. Is there anything you need, anything at all?"

She held my gaze as I shook my head in response. "Well, is there anything new you want to talk about with either case?" She read the confusion in my eyes and smiled. "The case of the crazed murderer or the case of the crazy rat infidel soon to be called your ex-husband."

I snorted. "Where do I even start? It's all bad. It's truly all bad. Del's getting all my stuff *and* his girlfriend, and I'm being taken to the cleaners. End of story." I'd told my woes to so many people in the past two days, I could recite them in my sleep. But it *did* take away my appetite. Not entirely a bad thing.

"That ain't right." Cliff was indignant.

"No, it ain't. But it ain't changing anytime soon either. And I don't know what else to tell you. I'm just trying to keep my eyes on the prize. Stay safe, sane, and available to Samantha, and keep putting one foot in front of the other. And then remember to wake up and keep doing it again the next day. But I'll tell you this, I'm blessed in the middle of this storm. Don't get me wrong. I hate everything that's happening. It seems so surreal. But in those moments when it's all going down in front of me, here's what I see—you. Both of you and all my amazing friends. Warm and loving and present and everything I need, just when I need it. And what kind of crazy great news is that?"

My heart opened wider as I recounted the truth of the blessings I'd experienced since my world turned upside down.

"Nearly as crazy as having that terribly good-looking, Italian, FBI guy in your house, waiting on you hand and foot to hear Maggie tell it." Georgi held a fork in the air for emphasis. She stabbed it in my direction. "*Aha!* Your face is redder than Cliff's shirt! What's going on? Details please." She put the fork down and leaned in. Cliff rolled his eyes and concentrated on his skillet.

"It's not like that. We're just friends, colleagues really. He's here on a case and helping me out at the same time. No big deal. Not a 'thing.' Not a 'thing' at all." My voice had risen, but I couldn't help myself. I was going for "natural" and ending up with excited half-shouts.

"Methinks the lady doth protest too much." Cliff was back in the game now too. "You could do worse, Jo. You should think about it."

Georgi and I stared at him like a snake on the kitchen floor. "Cliff!" We shouted his name in unison. We startled ourselves and laughed a good long time. And we kept it up through the skillets, egg-whites and all.

By the time we'd finished breakfast, it was nearly 11:30 a.m. Cliff wanted to head to the Farm and Fleet, while Georgi and I were seriously debating whether to take a quick cruise to Devil's Lake. The lake won, and we dropped him off at home and headed out of town.

Georgi angled herself toward me in the passenger seat. "Are you about ready to come back home? They don't deserve you down there in Illinois. You've already got a great start with your rustic cabin on the lake. By the time you and all of us finish punching it up, it's going to be a beautiful haven. What are you waiting for? Come home."

The roads had only been plowed once this morning, so I slowed to the speed limit as we hit Highway 113.

"I wish. I don't even know what home *is* anymore—a place of my own that isn't the same without me. Home like you and Cliff have made for all these years in Baraboo. I don't know where that is for me anymore."

The soothing sites of heavier brush signaled our arrival at Devil's Lake State Park, and we drove toward the south shore, easily navigating the winding, asphalt road and sharp turns of Snake Hill. We made our way to the bottom of the country road that runs next to the picturesque lake. Waves crashed against the rocks on this brilliant, December afternoon, and we drank in the majesty of the scene. I was glad I'd asked Cliff to check on my cabin three days ago. Georgi and I could devote our few hours to the beauty of the terrain before us.

"Water's pretty high again this year—been so much rain. You can still see signs of this fall's flooding here and there. The walkway's still covered in water." Georgi pointed to a grove of trees with the hint of a path submerged between them.

"When did they put that in? I like it, but this isn't exactly Atlantic City for crying out loud. What's next? A roller coaster?" I glanced at Georgi and winked as I navigated the SUV around the curves hugging the lake.

"How long's it been since you were home, girl? This thing's been functional for about two-and-a-half years now. Are you still driving around with your head in the clouds, missing everything in front of you? You were always looking for what might be up ahead. A new case just waiting around the bend."

"Yeah, maybe." The road led into the campground area. I slowed down as we drove through a deserted checkpoint.

"Maybe that's the gift behind this mess," Georgi said. "Ever wonder what else you might've missed with all your rushing through life?"

A long sigh was my only answer, and she wisely changed topics before I stopped talking completely.

"So, seriously. What are you gonna do now? Don't be mad at me for saying this, but they're looking for a sheriff here in Sauk County. Be like a part-time job for you. You could be our first female sheriff. You'd be a regular rock star, and half your old buddies are on the county board. Got a good feeling you'd be a shoe-in."

"Uh-huh. Wanna walk around the lake? Maybe take a hike, seeing as how it's turning into another one of these freakishly warm winter days?" I steered toward the parking area.

"Thought you'd never ask."

I eased into a spot near the beach, parking in a row with a half-dozen other cars. Most of them sported ski racks on the top. Wisconsin in the winter. I shut the car off and turned to Georgi. "You're not going to pull out a beer or anything, are you?"

"That was *your* thing if you remember right."

"Oh, yeah, good point. How 'bout we shut up and hike?"

Georgi jumped out of my SUV and closed the door. She took off ahead of me, walking toward the start of the path we'd hike. It took me a minute of rummaging around in the backseat to find my sturdiest pair of workout shoes and put them on. I had to move from a jog to a sprint to catch up with her. I was glad to see she had chosen one of the most challenging trails. I needed to get out more.

It took a little while for us to get back in sync. Once we did though, it brought back memories of perfect afternoons spent together in high school, matching long strides as we admired every hot boy in the park. We walked the length of the parking lot in silence, side-by-side, until it was time to begin our ascent.

CHAPTER 27

Georgi and I scrambled upward, slipping and sliding along the steep path, until we reached the top, just as the wind picked up. The view of the clouds rolling over the lake was breathtaking. We stood together to take it in, moving slowly to catch the beauty in all directions. She handed me a pair of binoculars, and I had just stepped into a clearing to find the best possible vantage point when I remembered I hadn't checked my work cell lately.

I pulled it out of my pocket and saw that I'd missed seven calls and five texts from three different people. It must've been ringing off the hook in the restaurant, but I couldn't hear it because of the noise. This could not be good. I punched in my voice-mail code and heard Nick's message first.

"Josie, call me back. Now." The six that followed were from him, Gino, and Mitch. My stomach tightened into knots. Mitch's message was next, and I knew she'd put it to me straight. And she did.

"Chief, there's no good way to say this. We've got trouble. Cal Terry's on the loose. He broke out of jail sometime early this morning. We don't know how he pulled it off, but we need to know where you are. Nick said you could be in danger."

I sat down hard on a smooth rock near the clearing as I listened to the rest of the messages in silence. Georgi slipped over to my side, watching me take in the news, call-by-call. I looked up at her and shook my head, not yet able to speak. Instead, I glanced at the three strong bars, showing on the phone's face, and punched in Mitch's number.

I listened to the details of this impossible reality without responding.

"Chief, you need to stay put. VICAP matched Terry's prints on your Christmas card to the Little Sister Serial Killer. You could be in trouble. You're not coming back to town for awhile."

"That's what you think. I'm on my way"

"You really can't do that right now. It's too dangerous. The feds are bringing in more manpower. Let us bring him in."

"I don't care. I hear you. I get it. But you're talking about my territory now. I'm not backing off. We're tracking him down, and I'm leading the charge. I'll see you at the station in two-, two-and-a-half hours max." I hit the END button, stuck the phone back into my pocket, and then looked up at my lifelong friend.

"You want to talk about it?"

I switched into cop mode. "I can't. I've got to go."

"Figured. You want me to call Cliff to come pick me up so you can leave from here?"

"That'd be great." I looked around at the clearing. *How much more daylight could I count on?*

"On it." She followed my gaze. Was she getting nervous? She dialed Cliff on the phone and told him to pick her up right away.

"We need to go. Now." I looked up at the dark clouds.

"Okay. Let's get moving then. Looks like we have a storm rolling in anyway."

"Georgi?"

"Yeah?"

"Thanks for understanding. It's my job."

She placed her hand on my shoulder, and our glances met for a moment. Her eyes were rimmed with fear, and I was unable to hold her gaze. I couldn't stop myself from studying the area. *How long had Terry been on the loose? Had I put us both at risk by coming here?*

The pine trees grimaced under a strong gust of winter wind, sending a faint whistling sound around the bluff. Goosebumps raced over my body. I grabbed Georgi's arm, and we faced the stony descent together. We'd watched plenty of sunsets from this very spot over the years, but nothing like the dark clouds full of a rare winter rain rolling toward us. As we skidded down the shadowy trail, a heavy threat hung in the air. Despite my cop's backbone, I was spooked.

We arrived back at the trail head right before a pounding rain drenched us both. Cliff was already in the parking lot, waiting for us with a golf umbrella, and bless his thoughtful heart, he handed me a brown paper lunch bag as we hurried to my car. I stole glances over my shoulder, and I caught Georgi doing the same thing.

"Didn't think I'd let you get away without a trip to the Square Tavern did you?"

"This what I think it is?"

"Oh, yeah, baby."

"Cliff, if you were available, I'd marry you myself. Sorry, Georgi."

The three of us embraced in the parking lot for a few minutes. The warmth of their friendship and the hearty, steak sandwich and potato fries from Cliff got me all the way home in less than two hours.

I might have broken a few speed limits, so the magnetic flashing light I placed on top of my car came in handy. The municipal plates didn't hurt either.

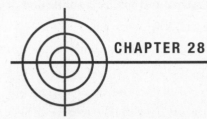

CHAPTER 28

By the time I pulled into my parking space at the station, my sense of foreboding had become unbearable. Tense nerves sent tremors of energy up and down my spine, and every muscle in my body seemed to have gone straight to fight or flight mode. Something else had happened. I could feel it in my bones.

Pushing past the bullpen, I headed straight to the conference room, where I recognized the voices of Nick, Mitch, and Gino arguing with someone. It sounded like a small army had set up camp in there.

Julie was in. On New Year's Eve. She didn't speak as I passed her cubicle. Her eyes were red and her skin splotchy. Not good. We nodded at each other as I strode past and stepped inside the conference room. I shut the door behind me.

I'd expected to see my friends, but I hadn't expected to see men in flak jackets emblazoned with FBI initials. Nick's face was grim. Definitely not good.

Everyone rose as I entered the room, including a man named Stone, according to his jacket, who sat on the other side of the table. I dropped into a chair, and everyone else followed suit.

I turned my attention to Stone when he cleared his throat. He offered me his hand. "Special Agent Harold Stone, Chief."

Rising from my seat, I shook his hand. I sat back down. Nick and Stone exchanged furtive glances, and I noted a subtle nod of the older man's head, deferring to Nick.

"Chief." The ominous feeling dug its claws in deeper when Nick addressed me by title. "Our problem's gone from bad to worse since we last spoke. We'll get to the details later, but what you'll want to know first is we have reason to believe this sick freak has grabbed another little girl." He paused to let that sink in.

I'd assumed as much from the grave looks on everyone's faces and the presence of the SWAT team. My professional self poured a molten mask over my face, even as my stomach grew rock hard, and my muscles tensed to the breaking point. Flight was no longer an option. It was time to fight. I nodded at him to go on, anger building like an army of warriors within me. Nick looked me steadily in the eyes. There was something even worse he had to tell me. My gaze turned hard, and I gave him a barely perceptible nod.

"Yours," he said. "Josie, it's Samantha. He's got Samantha."

My teeth clamped together so hard I thought they might break. I stared at him, willing away the tears that were coming to both of us.

Samantha. Taken. In danger because of me. I had to find her. *My girl. My fault.* She wasn't quite seven years old. Spunky and defiant, brilliant and deceptive. I loved that little girl more than life itself. And now, because of me and some sick fantasy Terry was nursing, he had taken her. I gathered my emotions before trusting my voice.

"When? How long ago?" My frantic thoughts made it almost impossible to focus. *My girl. My fault.*

Stop!

I had to stop being a mother and start being a cop. Samatha's life depended on it.

"Within the past three hours. We just learned about it forty minutes ago."

"Tell me." I gritted my teeth.

Stone took over the explanation. He had an annoying voice. "Near as we can tell, he and possibly an accomplice followed her to an afternoon Christmas pageant at her church. Snatched her in all the confusion. Seemed to be random until we figured out who she was."

"Is."

"Right. Sorry, Chief. We know now the kidnapping wasn't random. And the accomplice was a woman old enough to be his mother."

How did this happen? Where are you, Samantha? I know you're out there. Can you hear me? Talk to me! Lead me to you! I promise I'll find you. I'm coming for you, baby. Hang on.

Nick spoke in deep tones I'd never heard before, resonating with pain. "Tell her the rest, Stone."

"She was in the church pageant." His nasal voice grated my nerves.

"Yes, I know." I couldn't keep the anger from leaking out.

"Right. We've got witnesses putting him there, sitting through the whole thing, third row from the front." Stone kept his eyes neutral.

"Pretty bold. Why wasn't he afraid he'd be recognized? Why risk it?" I knew the answers to my questions even before they fell out of my mouth. Buster really was the Little Sister Serial Killer, and we'd underestimated him all along.

"Good disguise. Nice clothes. Dyed his hair. He totally changed his look. This guy's grown exponentially in timing and expertise." Stone shifted his weight.

"Give me your working profile for him, Nick. I'm up-to-date through the Mad Town incident and the trail he's left during the last year, but he's been in custody since then. Tell me about his movements since his escape."

"An insider—a guard—took a bribe. Terry had this all planned before he was ever arrested. We're going to get him, Josie. But we gotta move fast."

"Then why are we still here?"

"Because he's going to call you."

I knit my brows and looked around the office, noticing that a phone surveillance team had set up shop in a corner. A hostage negotiator stood by.

The enormity of the situation slowly sunk in. *Please let Sam be okay, God.* I could feel her. I could feel her panic. I had to snap into action and pull this team together and find my girl.

Stone cleared his throat to speak. "He studies up on unusual Big Sisters. Interesting ones—like you. How he makes his selections is still a mystery, but we've got some strong hunches. He's taken a very keen interest in you, Chief Oliver. And you fit the profile of his vics."

Not a profile I ever thought I'd fit. I needed Stone to finish this string of horrid news. "Go on. Let me hear it again."

"He seems to find attractive, successful, powerful women who have chosen to give back to the community by adopting a little girl. Some have been actual adoptees, some have been foster children, and some have been connected loosely through a church, synagogue, or temple. Others have been linked through the classic

Big Sister, Little Sister program, or something similar such as we have here. Doesn't matter. It's always the same. He uses the little girls to get to the women. Hasn't hurt a girl so far. We haven't figured out why he might have gone down that path yet, but we will. You know these first twelve hours are critical."

Not true. This first hour, these first minutes, right now was critical. Nick and I exchanged glances, and I knew he was thinking the same thing. My impotence in this moment when up against such a demonic force was terrifying.

"We've got to catch this evil monster. Now." I had to keep the team focused.

Just as Stone opened his mouth again, my desk phone rang.

CHAPTER 29

I let the phone ring three times, waiting for Stone to give me the nod. We hadn't had time to plan what I was going to say. I liked it better that way. I felt no allegiance to the FBI. This was just a job for him, a high profile case. This was family for me. For Nick, for Gino, and for Mitch. Things were going to go down my way, our way. I looked at each of them briefly before picking up the phone.

"Oliver."

"Hello, Chief. How are you today?" Terry's voice was bone-chillingly creepy. He had a slight southern accent, and he spoke in hushed tones.

"I'll be a lot better once I have your scrawny neck in my hands and you feel me crushing the life out of your useless—"

"Why, Josephine! You flatter me with your attention. If it's any consolation, Jo, I can't wait to get my hands on you either." His voice grew harder as he finished his last sentence, causing the muscles in Nick's jaw to tic.

"Listen, you soulless monster. You touch a hair on her head, and. . ." I knew I was breaking protocol the moment I opened my mouth.

"Oh, I will, Chief. I surely will. And then I hope to do the honors with you as well. Ta-ta for now."

The line went dead before I could find a way to lure him out any further. I'd lost my temper. I knew better. And I knew without asking that no trace had worked in that short amount of time. I'd netted no real information. By any standard, FBI or otherwise, I'd failed . . . miserably. *I'd failed Samantha.*

Stone scowled at me. "Well, that went well."

CHAPTER 30

Stone took this as his cue to impose a fifteen-minute break. Jerk. We had no time for breaks—not until my girl was home safe. I really wanted to put my hands around his throat and squeeze some sense into him. I'd been there less than an hour, and already I'd botched things up. I might've ruined everything. I might've cost us a life—not just any life—Samantha's.

I could *not* let that happen. I needed some time with my team to brainstorm. Maybe Stone's imposed break was a good idea.

"Let's take fifteen." I glanced at those people I trusted.

Memories of Samantha assailed me. The soft sound of her little voice whispering, "I love you, Jo," before dropping off to sleep during a camping trip. Her golden laughter the day I showed her where Scooter liked to be scratched. The shining hope in her eyes when I promised her life could be better than what she'd seen so far.

I waited until it was just the four of us—Nick, Gino, Mitch, and me. Julie slipped in with fresh coffee and bagels for everyone as soon as the door opened. She winked at me with tired eyes as she drove Stone and the SWAT guys out like a herd of cattle. I mouthed my thanks as she closed the door behind them.

"Nick, we need a plan and fast. I am not going to sit here while Samantha is in danger. We've got to get men out to the forest preserves, to the playgrounds, parks, maybe even to the old fairgrounds."

I didn't need to point out that I was listing what could be construed as likely body drops in our neck of the woods. Each area would offer plenty of room and isolation for Buster to do his evil work. I didn't know where else to start.

"We've covered that ground, Chief. We've got K-9 officers combing all those places. We're sending teams out to the savanna too." Mitch was already on the job, and I realized how much I'd discounted my team.

"I'm sorry. Of course you have. You love her too—all of you." I looked around at them, and tears surfaced as I locked eyes with Nick. We had to find a way to pull together so we could make best use of our considerable talent. I was failing them. We were failing *her*. I didn't know what else to do.

I did know, though, what the Little Sister Serial Killer had done to his victims. I didn't want to think about it. I couldn't. Nick stepped into the void my silence created.

"Look, we need to take a deep breath and be grateful for what we do know. Let's start there."

This sentiment was so unexpected that we all turned and stared at him. Gino, in particular, seemed impressed with Nick's suggestion at such a time as this. That was usually Gino's territory.

"For starters, let's remember that his last kill was *not* a little girl." Nick's words hit me like a bomb, and I turned away from him, eyes stinging. "No, listen to me. We're forgetting something. He has a pattern, a very distinct pattern. He isn't going to veer off of it now. This is too important. This could be the mother of all kills for him." Our confused faces seemed to disappoint him as he soldiered on. "Think about it. He plans his kills. He hasn't varied so far, and he's not going to vary now. Everything he's done up until he got clipped was precise."

I sucked in my breath as I finally understood where Nick was going with this. Sweet hope hung in the air.

Gino looked thoughtful. "So what you are saying, or better put perhaps, *not* saying, is that our *querida* Samantha is not the victim, but she is the bait."

"I agree." Mitch's quick joy turned to anger.

"It's *me* he's after."

"Yes." All three of them answered in unison.

I could almost see the pistons firing in each of our brains. Julie seemed to have sensed it too. She knocked twice and then opened the door, ushering in Stone and his team. A plan was forming in my mind. I wanted time alone with Mitch, Nick, and Gino to work it out in my war room, but I knew we'd have to settle for the FBI audience. Fair enough.

While we waited for another call, which might or might not come, every field team reported in, but they came up empty. We all pored over maps of the area, and then we started over. We couldn't keep walking through sludge like this. Samantha needed us—needed me. We'd learned nothing so far. Exhaustion wrapped itself around me like a shroud. Dark pictures of Samantha in the clutches of a madman gnawed at the fabric of my sanity. If she didn't make it—*no*. I refused to think about that.

Everything you are is everything you need to find her. Alive. Whoa! Where did that come from?

Peace and power streamed into me, ushering in that same strong presence of God. I breathed Him in like the sweetest fragrance, growing stronger with every breath.

Suddenly, my mind cleared. From the looks and responses of my three *amigos*, I could tell we were all having a similar experience.

We were on fire—planning and working together like a crew of highly trained combat operatives.

"Okay, what do we know about Samantha? Where does she live? What does she love? How does she think? How does she respond?" Nick's simple questions seemed to unlock parts of me that the tension in the room had sealed shut. I answered them as simply and rapidly as he threw them out. Mitch captured all the information on the white board.

"She lives on the south side with her foster family. She loves animals, especially cows. And ice cream and chocolate butter-cream frosting. Pea soup made in my blender. She's scrappy. And smart. She's quick-witted. She's strong. She's a survivor."

"Yes, keep it up," Nick said. "What would she have been wearing at the pageant?"

"A robe. She wanted to be a camel, or a cow, or a donkey, and she was mad they wouldn't let her. She had to settle for being a wise man. Her stubborn streak made me laugh. I was proud of her for standing up for herself, so I . . ."

As I realized what I was about to say, I nearly lost my hope. I choked up. Mitch stopped writing on the board. Everyone stared at me.

"So I bought her a little stuffed cow for her to put under her robe during the show—the best of both worlds." The excitement I'd generated died down. But I hadn't gotten to the good part yet. "The stuffed animal's official name was Bert, but she wanted it to be a girl, so she named her Ethel. Ethel is a mini-Furkinz."

"A Furkinz! The one you took to the vet and had him embed a computer chip inside of, just like you did with Scooter?" Mitch popped up from the corner of the table.

"Oh dear God—I did! I can't believe you remembered that.

She wanted to be just like me, so I took her and Ethel to the vet and we played make believe by putting a real animal tracking chip inside her Furkinz." A ray of hope flooded through me.

"You know what this means, don't you?" Mitch stepped in front of me, clasping her hands together in front of her mouth and looking up at me with moist eyes.

"Best thirty-five bucks I ever spent. We can track it!"

I reached for the phone and dialed. Nick was already speaking quietly on his cell phone, and Gino typed on an iPad that I didn't know he had. Finally, I heard a voice on the other end of the line.

"Computer Crimes Commission. Bentley, here."

It took Bentley less than five minutes to call me back after I'd explained what we were after. He'd somehow gotten the serial number of the chip embedded in the Furkinz and confirmed that it did, indeed, give off faint signals. I knew she'd have it with her. She took it everywhere.

Bentley took the liberty of narrowing down possible signals. The faint signal had a distinct signature, detectable by new equipment he'd designed and was working on patenting. While he couldn't track down the exact location of the Furkinz, he had isolated a three-mile radius on the west side of Chain of Lakes State Park.

I knew the area well—had ridden my horse over that terrain many times. Isolated, with thick, matted pines growing every which way, it would provide the ideal cover, even in the dead of winter. A few hunting cabins dotted the countryside up there. It made all the sense in the world. Now if we could just narrow down the three-mile radius fast enough.

We agreed to a hasty plan as Mitch contacted the canine teams and redeployed them. We were going to make it. I could feel it. An electric buzz seemed to emanate from my inner being as we raced out the station doors. The bright moonlight was a shock to my system, as was the unexpected blast of warm, moist air. I'd forgotten about the odd weather we'd been having, regretting the thick layers I'd piled on under my Kevlar vest.

But personal comfort was a luxury I didn't have at the moment. Would we find her in time? We had to. Desperation fueled my need for speed as Mitch and I jumped into my car and squealed out behind Gino and Nick.

CHAPTER 31

As we crouched in the woods near the cabin, my lower abdomen pressed up against the unyielding leather of my gun belt, a small roll of fat leaking out of the bottom of the Kevlar vest encircling my upper body. We'd been wearing this gear longer than I wanted, but I didn't care. It fueled my anger and gave me a sense of power.

Nick's nudge snapped me back to full attention. Stone was on my left, and Nick squatted on my right. Each clasped an AR aloft and in ready position. I held my trusty Glock in my right hand.

A SWAT team crouched behind us ready to storm the building. All in all, power was on our side. Firepower, manpower, enough power to take out this evil monster. The breaching team silently moved into place, shouldering their battering ram as if it weighed no more than a fringed rug. The lead man gave me a thumbs-up and waited for my signal to charge. Thanks to Nick, the Feds had given up trying to wrestle command away from me for the takedown. This was personal. *My* girl. *My* case. Mine to win, lose, or die trying.

There were no windows on the heavy wooden door of the cabin, and I was confident we hadn't given ourselves away. The terrible pressure of knowing every second was life or death for my little girl bore down hard on me. And she would be *my* little girl; she *was* my little girl. Pending divorce or no, the paperwork would start tomorrow. The adoption was a done deal in my heart. With God by my side, I lifted my head, gave the nod to the breaching team, and unleashed hell on the monster inside.

Everything seemed to happen at once like a well-choreographed dance. The moves went down exactly as we'd planned on the drive over. The door gave way after one swing. I was the first one into the room, with Stone and Nick on my six and dozens of cops and agents right behind them. We located the perp in the back of the living room, up against the wall, bent over a bench full of metal. A little heap rested on a dirty mat on the floor, at a ninety-degree angle from the killer. *Please let her still be alive.*

The entire operation unfolded in a smooth, free flow of room-clearing tactics. Men peeled off in all directions, securing the small dwelling in seconds. My team and every other rifle bore down on Terry. I kept my Glock trained on him in a two-handed stance, eyes furtively glancing from the tiny figure on the mat on the floor next to Terry.

Nick ordered Terry to put his hands on his head and stand up. When the perp turned around, a strong, terrifying sense of evil swirled around me as his eyes locked onto mine. I might've been okay if he hadn't done the two things at once. He smiled. He smiled and then he lunged for my girl. Samantha screamed and her terror echoed through my heart, spurring me forward. The minute he bent his knee and sloped toward my Samantha lying helpless on the mat before him I squeezed the trigger. Twice in rapid succession.

The first shot was low, hitting him in the knee. He crumpled onto the concrete, mercifully falling away from my girl. The second shot caught him in the shoulder, disabling him entirely. I stepped over to Samantha, still in the classic two-handed shooter stance, stopping when I stood directly over her.

Her little chest moved with ragged breaths. Paramedics were ushered in and surrounded her. I stepped away from her to give them enough room. I looked down upon her shuddering frame and thanked the God I did not understand for keeping her alive.

And then I lifted my head.

From somewhere deep inside, I emitted the growl of a she-wolf.

I trained my Glock on the evil man on the ground before me. His eyes were black orbs. He couldn't talk, but he smirked. I inched forward, chambered another round, wanting nothing more than to pump him full of lead until he stopped smirking, but Nick gripped my shoulder to stop me.

I holstered the Glock and sank to my knees by Samantha's side. The medics opened their circle for me. Samantha's fearful eyes locked on mine, and she whimpered as she reached for me.

I took her shaking hand and looked into her eyes. "It's all right, sweetheart. You're safe now. I'm here." I kissed her head gently and smoothed her hair. "We're all here for you, Sam. He can't hurt you anymore."

She clutched my hand to her chest and started to cry. The paramedics had started an IV, and as the sedative took effect, her body relaxed into me, her grip loosening. I held her hand until the sedation pulled her under and reluctantly allowed the medics to prep her to leave.

I rose and turned around, glad to see Buster had been removed. Stone and Nick exchanged glances of relief. I knew I'd be in trouble for today. Possibly big trouble, given the size of the audience. But I didn't care. Totally worth it. I cleared my throat and turned to face the music. We had done our jobs and got it right.

CHAPTER 32

While exploring the killer's lair, we made a sad discovery—the body of a woman, badly mutilated. Compassion and sorrow walked with us as we searched for any other victims. My heart was with Samantha though. I needed to be with her when she woke up.

Nick tapped me on the shoulder. "Let's go."

He took my field notebook, closed it, and pointed a gloved finger toward the door. I followed him out and let him lead me to the car. Exhaustion seeped out of my every pore. He hugged me with tenderness. My arms folded around him, and the warmth of his body gave me a sense of renewed energy. He kissed me on the forehead and gently tucked me into the seat.

"She's going to be okay Josie. And so are we." He kissed me again and then went to his side of the car and got in. He sat there, taking me in with those intelligent eyes.

He reached out a hand, and I took it in mine, placed it near my lips and kissed his knuckles one by one, keeping my eyes on him. "I know Nick. I feel it too. And all I can tell you is not yet. I'm married. For now." I closed my eyes and gave my head a shake.

My uniform pants were encrusted with mud and filth and worse; my hands were smudged with who knows what, and I'd touched things and people I'd rather not think about. And that was only me. Only God knew where those four knuckles I'd just kissed had been this evening, and the whole thing struck me as funny. I laughed so hard I teared up. I couldn't explain it to Nick, and he gave up looking at me as he drove us to the hospital.

We were ushered straight to the emergency room. I grabbed Nick's hand and pulled him near me.

"Nick, I'm scared to death to see her. What if she blames me?" My voice broke. "What if she'd . . . what if . . ." Shudders worked their way up from my gut, and my shoulder blades trembled.

Nick pulled me into him. "Josie, no, no, no. You saved her life. She knows that. You saved her life. You love her. She loves you, and she needs you. Now go to her." He pulled back and kissed me on the forehead for the third time in ten minutes, giving me a gentle push in the direction of her room.

Nick veered off to get an update on Sam's condition while I made a beeline to her bedside. Her small frame was sheathed in blankets, and a bandage covered her right cheek. She slept peacefully. The softly beeping monitors around her indicated her tiny body was stable. I'd tried so hard to give her what she needed most—a loving mother figure—and I'd nearly gotten her killed.

I placed a trembling hand on her head. Her eyes remained closed. Her breathing didn't change. *Please, God. Please take care of my little Samantha. Please heal her.* I didn't know what to say, how to pray. I willed her to get better, to forgive me. What kind of mother could I possibly be to her? I kissed her on the forehead and smoothed back her hair.

Nick grasped my shoulder and came in close enough to whisper while looking down at Sam. "It's all good, Josie. It's all good." He punctuated the news with a quick kiss on my ear lobe.

I pulled away with a start. "What did they tell you?"

"She's exhausted, she's badly bruised, and she suffered a

sprained wrist. While the SOB did rough her up pretty badly, he didn't . . . he didn't . . ." Nick turned his face away and gulped in air.

I turned and put my arms around him. "It's all good, Nick. It's all good." I reached up and kissed him on the cheek and rested my chin on his shoulder as I held him. "My little girl is going to be just fine. And so are we. More than fine." I stepped away from him and turned to look at Samantha, my little miracle girl, still clutching the cow.

I knew she would triumph over all that had been done to her. She had to. And we'd all be there for her as she faced whatever trauma the demon had inflicted on her spirit. My face relaxed, and I tipped my head up in silent thanks to a God I barely knew. I leaned down to brush Sam's bangs up and gently kissed her forehead again.

A small man wearing a large DCFS badge pushed the curtain aside. The man's eyes met mine, and we smiled at each other.

"Hey Marty." Samantha's social worker shook my hand in his grizzly-like grip. He had a ferocious demeanor, but his heart beat for his kids. Samantha would be in good hands in my absence. "Take good care of her."

"Go take care of business, Chief." His voice was raspy, and the look in his eyes was fierce.

I left the hospital, walking beside Nick with a much lighter heart and an iron resolve. "Let's get to the station. Pronto."

I zipped up my coat as we left the hospital. The wind had shifted out of the north, and the temperature had dropped.

Nick kept his hands in his pockets. "Babe, at least go home and catch a quick nap. I know you want to be there to tie up loose ends, but you need to go home and take a shower and a half-hour nap." He ended his mini-lecture with a yawn.

A shower and a nap might just be the ticket to calming my nerves and steeling myself for the work ahead. The dark streets streamed by as he drove.

"Guys like him could be out there by the dozen, Nick. How do you live knowing that? What keeps you so, so, I don't know, so you?"

He smiled and placed a hand on my shoulder. "You, babe—you." He dropped me off at home, and I showered before catching an hour's nap and returning to the station. Nick was already there.

Later on that morning, I tried to review the crime-scene photos, but it was too much for me. I had to leave the folder behind and find a bathroom in a hurry. I kept seeing myself, or worse yet, Samantha, in that poor woman's place. The brutality was unimaginable—a depth of wickedness I couldn't fathom.

Evil had entered my territory, and there'd been nothing I could do to prevent it. I was doing my best to be present in the aftermath, taking back control of my station, my village, my world, and standing up for my officers in the midst of the horror. It was the hardest work I'd ever done.

"Josie, you're gonna want to be in on this." Nick's eyes narrowed as they met mine. I followed the slight nod of his head toward the interview room. *He was in there.* The cold steel of the doorknob awoke the cop in me.

Cal Terry, aka Buster, looked up and tried to rise from his chair, but as soon as he moved, two guards emerged from the shadows and pushed him back into his seat. His hands were cuffed at the wrist, and he was chained to the floor by an ankle cuff. A receding hairline littered with wisps of what may have once been blondish hair rendered him unassuming. I tried to figure out where the gravitational pull toward him was coming from. He was like a vortex of evil.

His head was bandaged, and one cornflower-blue eye was swollen nearly shut. I sat down at the table next to Nick. Terry stared past me as he spoke.

"In the South, we rise for women, ma'am. Especially beautiful women."

"So, Buster, why don't we pick up where we left off?" Nick snapped his notebook open and shut a few times, trying to get the perp's attention, but Terry seemed to have set sail for his own world. His eyes hadn't left the wall over my shoulder.

I crossed my arms and leaned back in my chair. "What, you think this is a bad first date? Why don't you tell me all about yourself. Let's start with the lady in blue. And don't leave anything out."

"I already told your associates my story, ma'am. And I think you know. You were there. You came to me after all. I knew you would. He said you would." His voice was high and soft, and he whispered half of what he said as though he wasn't sure if it should be said. "But I'll tell you again if you like. Fact is, I'll tell you anything you want."

His Adam's apple moved up and down as he spoke. His slight southern accent added a sense of menace to his words.

"Why don't you start at the beginning? With the shower." Nick's voice was impatient.

Buster's face turned bright red, and his arms developed a tremor. A strong odor wafted our way, and I couldn't tell if it was fear or death. Nick and I exchanged glances.

I nodded at the perp. "Please. Tell me your story, Mr. Terry."

"I already told them, ma'am." He jerked his head, tearing his eyes away from the wall and staring straight down at the table in front of him.

"And now you can tell me." The sound of my voice moved him, and he bent his neck further toward the table.

"It happened in the shower," he said.

"*What* happened?"

"He told me. He told me everything."

"Who did?"

"God."

"God?"

"God."

"In the shower?"

"Yes."

His voice was now a whisper, and I fought myself from leaning forward to hear more clearly.

"What exactly did God tell you in the shower? Did God tell you to do something? Talk to someone? What did he tell you?"

"He told me all about her." He shifted uncomfortably in his seat, intensifying the odor. Fear. Definitely fear.

I stared at him.

"The governor's wife." He looked up at me as he spoke, his cruel eyes sparkling. "The woman at the table. Wearing the blue wrap."

"What did God tell you about her?"

"That she was bad. And God is good."

"What else did he tell you?"

"That he is good and she was bad, and because he is, she cannot be."

"What do you think he meant by that?"

"That she must die. I must kill her for him. To cleanse her so that she could stand in his presence in the afterlife."

"What was his voice like? God's voice."

His head snapped up at the question. He looked me in the eye, and his lips curled into a sneer. Evil burned brightly in his foul eyes.

"You don't believe me."

"I might."

"You don't believe me. You don't hear him."

"Is he here now?"

He snorted and shook his head violently as if to expel a demon or two. "Yes. Of course."

"Is he talking to you now?"

"No. He's listening."

"What is he hearing?" A chill ran through me.

"He is hearing what I will and will not tell you."

"Will you tell me what else he said to you in the shower?"

He paused. His eyes glazed over, and thirty seconds of silence passed before he responded. "Yes."

"All right, Mr. Terry. What did God tell you to do about the bad woman when you were in the shower?"

"You won't like it."

"Try me." Bands of steel tightened around my temples.

"He told me to enjoy her."

"And did you?"

"Oh, yes. I enjoyed her very much."

I felt lightheaded and began to see the faintest glimmer of stars sparkling on and off in the distance. My temples constricted, and my stomach tightened. I'd already seen the crime-scene photos and both heard and read his initial confession. I didn't need to hear any more. I pushed myself away from the metal table and nodded toward the one-way glass as I rose to my feet. This interview was over.

CHAPTER 33

I had an initial court date the following Monday morning. The events of the past several days and spending time with Samantha had taken up every spare ounce of energy I had. Mercifully, it left me with no time to think about my pending divorce and my newly impoverished state. I'd been acting and thinking like a single mother for days. How did that happen?

My newfound peace lasted through the court appearance. Of course, the fact that Del had not deigned to appear didn't hurt. I wasn't looking forward to seeing him again. Facing his lawyer proved to be annoying enough in a very costly way. I listened half-heartedly as two grown men argued like preteens over a bunch of stuff they didn't own.

What had we become? I hung around long enough to be polite after the judge issued a continuance, and then I lit out of there before my attorney could wind back up. Gino and I had a lunch date I didn't want to miss.

I'd been thinking a lot about all the life-altering events during the past month and especially about the encounter in Maya's office. That seemed to be the first time I could remember a conscious awareness of God, and I deeply desired to understand what it all meant. Gino was probably the only person I could bring it to who could help me sort it all out.

We'd planned to meet at a favorite Italian restaurant in Kenosha, just over the state line. He was already there when I drove up, late, but earlier than my usual version of late. I hoped I'd get some clemency for coming here straight from divorce court. The big man stood up to hug me. After ordering a plate of bruschetta for starters, I gave him a sterile version of my morning and then got down to what was really on my mind.

"Gino, I think I might be cracking up."

"*Tu, m'hija? Tu?* Yes, you are and have always been a little crazy—*es cierto*—but only in the most amusing of ways."

It all came tumbling out. My moments, as I'd come to think of them—the dark presence that had plagued me early on, my first encounter with God, and all the sharp twinges of just seeming to know things before they happened.

Gino took it all in, asking me detailed questions along the way, as if I were the most interesting patient ever and he was trying to diagnose a rare condition.

"And this presence, how often do you sense Him with you?"

"A lot of the time, Gino. Ever since. I don't know—maybe since the night of the crash, when life as I knew it came to a screeching halt. And then in a very real way that day on Maya's couch. Something's not right with her, Gino. I felt as if God was actually there to protect me from her. I know that sounds crazy, G—"

"Is He here with you now, *m'hija?*"

"Very much so. He's all around us. I can feel Him."

At this, Gino bowed his head, closed his eyes, and seemed to go somewhere else. He didn't say anything, and his lips weren't moving, so I didn't think he was praying. I hung in there, waiting for him in silence. Still not my strong suit. I looked at my watch and mindlessly drummed my finger on the table between us. Gino grasped my finger and lifted it from the table, shushing me. I rolled my eyes and waited.

"I saw that!" His chocolate eyes glistening with love steadied me.

"You are a very blessed woman. I must now tell you of the love of God and of His wonderful plan for your life. And today I am certain that you will be able to hear me. First, you must tell me more of this doubt with which you are struggling."

"I can't, Gino. You won't like how it sounds. I don't like how it sounds. It's all pretty irreverent. I'm not sure you or God will want to hear it."

"And that is where you are wrong, *m'hija*. That is the beauty of our God. Before you even form the words you feel you must share, He already knows what you're going to say. And He has forgiven you before you even knew you needed Him to do so. So speak. Share of your doubts." Gino turned stalwart eyes to me.

"Here's the thing, G. If God is this all-seeing, all-knowing kind of God, then where was He when I needed Him? Where was He with Del? Why didn't He stop Del from ruining my life? Huh? Wanna try to tell me that?" The force of my anger surprised me. "And don't even get me started on what kind of a loving God would let that monster kill so many women, destroy so many lives. What kind of love is that?"

He watched me intently and patiently. When it was clear I was done for the moment, he took both of my hands in his.

"*M'hija*, I will not pretend to understand the depth and breadth of our God and why He does what He chooses, or why He does not do what He does not choose to do. It is a mystery to me as well.

"There is much pain in this world, and *si*, He could surely stop it if He so desired. But He is a God of great love and of great mercy, and He longs for us to choose Him on our own. How could you love a God who was more of a genie to you? Who granted your every wish and fulfilled your every desire? Where is the faith in that? But that is not the God of the universe. That is not the God we serve."

"But—"

"*M'hija*, let us return now to you. He has been calling you, waiting for you. He has allowed you to suffer through some terrible losses and struggles. And I know He could put a stop to these this instant if it would please Him to do so. But something much greater is happening." He slowly turned his water tumbler and then pushed it away from his plate.

"I have seen how the Holiest of Holies has been using your pain to soften your heart, to open up your spirit to His presence. You are His precious alabaster vase. And your beauty only grows as He breaks you—as you allow His presence to transform your sorrow into joy and your struggles into victories. In the breaking of His alabaster vase there is much joy and beauty."

My knit brows and grimace spoke before I did. "I don't understand what you're saying. Why am I a vase? What's precious about being a vase?"

"Ah, let me tell you a story. There was once a great and mighty emperor who lived in a very impressive castle, and he liked to surround himself with only the most beautiful people and things. His prized possession was the most beautiful alabaster vase the world had even seen. One day, a small boy came to seek permission to look upon the beautiful vase. The emperor granted this permission, and the little boy was grateful. But the boy accidentally tripped and fell into the pedestal that held the exquisite vase, causing it to tumble to the ground." Gino's eyes grew soft as he spoke. He picked up the root beer he'd ordered and took a long draught.

"As it fell, the emperor panicked, and he ordered his servants to save it, but they could not. The vase crashed onto the marble floor and was broken into a thousand pieces. The emperor was furious and ordered the boy to be arrested for his clumsiness. But then, the emperor noticed the strangest, most beautiful fragrance he had ever experienced coming from the precious oil that had poured out when the vase was destroyed. This precious oil and its beautiful fragrance permeated the entire castle, transforming it into a far more beautiful palace.

"And so it is with you, *m'hija*. God has allowed some terrible things to happen in your life, but He has made you far more beautiful because of it."

I had teared up halfway through Gino's story. He gently wiped my tears with a napkin and then tossed two twenties on the table. He rose to his feet, holding his hand out to me. I took it, and we walked out of the restaurant.

"I know a place that is perfect for you at this time. A little chapel in the wilderness not ten minutes from here. I will drive." It wasn't a question.

He held open the passenger door for me, and I slipped inside his car. We ended up at a little wooden church, standing out in the middle of a corn field. We stepped over downed corn stalks on our way to the steps and found the door open. I followed Gino in and sat with him in one of the smallish, straight-backed pews. I was in the strong presence of God once again, awash in His majesty and peace.

After long moments of silence, Gino spoke. "*M'hija*, this much is not so complicated. In the beginning, He was. From the beginning, He created us. He created the world. He created mankind to reflect His own face, to glorify Him, to give testimony to Him as the Creator. You can bring yourself back to the story in the beginning? *El Jardin*?"

"Yeah, sure. I mean, I think. Wait, you mean the Garden of Eden?"

He nodded.

"Are you kidding me? I know the deal. God creates the universe. God gets lonely and creates man. Big mistake. He should have created woman first, and He quickly figures that out. So man gets lonely, longs for a two-footed friend, and God creates woman. Woman hangs with man, hears about how wonderful he is and how happy he's keeping the flora and the fauna, and this makes the woman hungry.

"Man ignores woman, opting instead to keep yammering on about how great he is. Woman pretends to listen, grabs an apple, politely shares it with man, and things go downhill in a jiffy. Turns out God is a lover of both apples and obedience. God confronts man. Man lies and blames woman. Everybody stops talking to each other. Bad things happen, and they've been happening ever since. So? You're not really setting me on fire over here. I don't see your point."

"If you were not so busy creating your own stories, I would be pleased to continue." His accent was getting thicker by the second. He was becoming very emotional. For Gino.

"*M'hija*, if I could be at just this moment a lover of the women, and you were sitting there, just as you are, looking so very beautiful, with the *espiritu santo* shining so brightly through you and present all over you, I would fall in love with you. But as His ways are not our ways, I will just love you all the same."

My heart was so constricted that I couldn't speak. I felt the strongest sense of God's love and belonging as his soft, brown eyes met mine. "But you must hear the best part. Though we have all sinned and fallen short of the glory of God, even so He loves you and calls you to Him."

My eyes clouded over. "But all I do is fail. I failed at my marriage. I failed at protecting Samantha. What could God possibly want with me?"

"*M'hija*, this is when He wants you most. He sent His Son to die for you that you might be saved from your own failures, from your self-condemnation. 'If you confess your sins, He is faithful and just to forgive you and to cleanse you from all unrighteousness.' He has more for you."

Blood drained from my face as more memories of past failures came to mind. "But how do I walk with the weight of all I've done? How can God want me?"

"He loves you, *m'hija*. He forgives you. He cleanses you and makes you as white as the snow. He does not see as we see. His eyes are kind and wide and all knowing. He sees beyond today. Beyond any one moment in time. He loves you and has so much more for you—so much left for you to do. Here. For Him. And for others." His soft eyes shone with life.

"Like Samantha." I closed my eyes and let the truth come to me. When I opened them, Gino stood before me, praying. I bowed my head and joined him. *I know My sheep and My sheep know me* rang through my mind as my spirit snuggled into the arms of the God of Ages, my Rock, my Love, the Most High God.

His nearness drew me to Him, and I found my home in Him. Love and joy rang through me, flooding me with a deep, irretrievable love for Him. I moved into the aisle and sank to my knees.

My arms lifted up to the heavens, and I closed my eyes and sang an old Bible camp song that sprang into mind.

Gino joined me mid-song. His shoulder brushed mine as he knelt beside me.

For the second time in weeks, months, years maybe, I felt a true sense of belonging and a solid purpose in my life. I felt as if I'd come home as I worshipped at the feet of God. The horrors of the past several days fell away as I prayed as best I could to the God I'd somehow always known, but never met. Until this afternoon.

CHAPTER 34

My over-zealous Glock action netted me a three-day suspension, so I spent all the time the courts and Samantha's foster family would allow me with her. Her resilience amazed me. I would be forever grateful for the confident way she looked into my eyes.

Her hand was always locked in one of mine when we left the house. Most of our time together was spent taking little trips around town, visits to ply Scooter with carrots, playing her favorite games, and baking cookies and cakes together. I was getting a handle on the parenting thing.

After winter break, Samantha stayed full time with her foster family until our case wound its way through the courts. I shifted my attention to work and spent my first day back in the office, enjoying what looked like a few days of relative peace and quiet.

I had nothing on my schedule, with the exception of a mandatory meeting with the one and only Nick Vitarello. He'd actually scheduled a meeting on my work calendar through Julie—a first. Was there another case he wanted my help with? The clock seemed to slow down and almost stop as I waited for him to show up, so I pulled up annual personnel reviews in an attempt to get it moving again by trying to engage my mind in real work.

Nick's signature knuckle-rap announced his arrival. *Saved by the knuckles.* I shut the report file down and rose to greet him, butterflies in my stomach. In January no less. I opened my office door. Nick stood there in all his glory, wearing Armani cologne and a boyish grin.

"Aren't you going to invite me in, beautiful?" His velvety-brown eyes sparkled.

I stepped back, inviting him in with a wave of my hand. He looked good enough to eat. For a moment I thought of reciting the Lord's Prayer just to keep my mind focused on things above and not on the beauty and the wonder that was Nick.

He walked over to stand in front of one of the leather club chairs facing my desk. Not at all like him. What was going on? I started to sit behind my desk.

"Ah, Jo, would you mind joining me over here?" His gesture suggested I join him on the other side of my desk. *Jo? Did he just call me Jo?* For one insane instant I wondered if something else horrible had happened to someone I loved.

I walked numbly to the chair next to his and sat down. He waited until I was settled in before sitting next to me. I looked at him expectantly. "Nick?"

His eyes softened as he looked into my mine. Oceans of strength, and hope, and kindness swam before me in them. I wanted to dive in and bask in that warmth with him forever. He closed his eyes for a few seconds and then opened them again and cleared his throat.

"So, Jo, I set up this meeting today for a very special reason. I wanted to have a conversation about us." *Us? He wants to have a conversation about us? And he schedules one? Who does that?*

"Go on." I decided to play it cool . . . if I could. You know, the less-is-more approach. There were so many ways any conversation about "us" could go.

"Josie." He took my right hand and held it in both of his, sending jolts of love and peace rocketing through me. "You are the most wonderful woman in the world. I admire everything about you. Your tender heart, your love for God, your search for justice, your wisdom, the warrior in you. All of it, all of you. I admire all of you. And I want more." His eyes were clear. As they stared into mine, I saw hope and a future.

And then, just as suddenly, a black wave of terror threatened to crush me. A Mac truck sat on my chest. My pulse raced, and I wondered if Nick could hear it. I bowed my head.

God, I need you now! Please take my hand and lead me through this moment of fear and into Your glorious light. Here is this wonderful man declaring his love for me, and I need You to keep things straight, to show me Your ways, to let me know the right next step.

I lifted my head and looked at the man beside me. I breathed God into the moment. My heartbeat slowed, and my nerves settled to a dull roar. *Perfect love casts out all fear.* I smiled into those soft, brown eyes.

"Nick, I've loved you since forever, and I'll love you til the grave. As much as I love you, I have to say I love the God who made you more, and I seek to obey Him first before all others. And one thing I can tell you, I am a married woman, and until or unless that fact changes, there's nothing more that can be done or said between us."

My valiant attempt at putting God first and Nick a close second had not gone bone deep. My eyes were still speaking to him in love. I drew them away from the shining love I saw staring back at me and looked back at our hands clasped together. Something on the inside of his right wrist caught my eye—a smudge of dirt?

"Relax, beautiful. I'm not saying I want to marry you . . . *yet.* I'm just saying I want to be the first in line when you're ready to entertain the thought. I'll leave the rest up to the man upstairs." Nick drew my hand to his lips and kissed it softly. His sleeve fell away, revealing an exquisitely shaped cross. I stared at it, frowning.

"Nick? Is that a tat?" I ran my index finger the length of it. *When had he gotten inked? And why?*

He nodded, pulling his jacket up enough to show the rest of it. Something was written in tiny black script, but I couldn't make it out. *Numbers? An abbreviation maybe?* I cocked an eyebrow at him.

"From now on, let no one cause trouble for me. For I bear on my body the brandmark of Jesus. Galatians 6:17. Let's just say Gino and I spent a little time on our knees at a chapel in the woods recently."

My heart raced again. Waves of joy cascaded over me. I wanted to skip around the room like a little kid. I bowed my head and thanked the God of the universe. Then, in my mind's eye, I saw myself alone in a meadow. The sun went down around me, and the heavens opened up, and a beam of otherworldly light shone all around me, connecting me to God in all His glory. He was a shining light of power and love and every virtue packed into one magnificent being. I was a minor expression of Him, shining with a powerful light of my own, connected to Him with my heart and soul.

God reached down from heaven and took my hand in His. I looked up at Him in love and trust and awe. I realized that next to Him stood another being of light and beauty and power and strength, also connected from the heart to His light and love.

The power and majesty of God shifted again, and the other being took shape as a man, lit brightly from within, standing beside Him. I couldn't see his features, but I knew the other being was my Nick. Then the beautiful beings turned to face the future and walk toward God together.

The vision faded and I opened my eyes. I tugged my hand free of his and spread my fingers out wide. My wedding band and engagement ring were still solidly in place. Nick took my hand, drew it to his mouth, and brushed his lips lightly against each finger. He paused on my ring finger. Then he bent it carefully, making the ring as prominent as possible. He studied the rings, and then he traced the faint outline of a bruise on the inside of my wrist with his finger. His finger trailed back up to my hand, and then he carefully bent the rest of my fingers until he'd formed my hand into a fist.

"I love you, Josie. All of you. Josie the warrior, Josie the lover of small children, and now, Josie the woman of God. I don't know what it all means, or where it will lead us. I don't need to know that today. Having you, having your friendship, is enough for today. And tomorrow. After that, only God knows. And that's enough for me." He gently released my hand.

The glorious warmth of him radiated through me. I placed my hand gently on the side of his face and nodded. Hope, sweet hope, glittered in his eyes like a beacon in the night.

ACKNOWLEDGMENTS

In the words of C. S. Lewis, I feel "lucky beyond my desserts" for the love and faithfulness of my family and friends who buoyed me throughout this magnificent debut journey. Special thanks to Margo and Joe, and Jodie and Carl for generating key character studies and ideas. More special thanks to my beautiful niece Catherine—a better writer by far—and to her equally beautiful sisters for sharing their delight with me along the way. Really special thanks to my warrior nephew, Dan, who taught me how to fight and which weapons to use for which battles—especially when you want to win.

Forever gratitude to Ruth Wagley, Dave Finger, and Gay Meads for reading and improving countless editions in the early days, and to Pete Finger for joining me in the celebrations.

Erynn Newman kept one hand on my shoulder while sharing her supernatural editing gifts, and I am grateful. Her work improved mine.

Thank you, Kit Tosello, and the Deep River Books publishing team, for getting me to the church on time.

Connect with the author:
www.CatherineFinger.com